POWER OF FIVE

POWER OF FIVE, BOOK 1

ALEX LIDELL

DANGER BEARING PRESS

ALSO BY ALEX LIDELL

Young Adult Fantasy Novels
TIDES
FIRST COMMAND (Prequel Novella)
AIR AND ASH
WAR AND WIND
SEA AND SAND

SCOUT
TRACING SHADOWS
UNRAVELING DARKNESS

TILDOR
THE CADET OF TILDOR

New Adult Fantasy Romance
POWER OF FIVE (Reverse Harem Fantasy)
POWER OF FIVE
MISTAKE OF MAGIC

SIGN UP FOR NEW RELEASE NOTIFICATIONS at
www.subscribepage.com/TIDES

PROLOGUE

River

"No," River told the magic pulsing through the wet earth beneath his palm. Not that the magic much cared for River's opinion. "Bloody no. That cannot be our fifth."

Stepping up beside him, River's quint brothers, Tye, Coal, and Shade—the latter in his wolf form—stared down from Mystwood's overlook to watch a mortal girl of about twenty push a wheelbarrow toward a compost pile. Her lush hair was a fiery brown hue that toyed with the sun's rays as the girl went about her work, dumping off her load of manure and pushing the wheelbarrow back toward the stable.

The estate on which the girl labored sprawled daringly close to the border to Mystwood, the dense forest separating the mortal lands from the fae's Lunos territory. Unsurprisingly, minus a handful of inns and taverns catering to the more

1

curious mortals—or lost ones—the closest village lay a full day's ride away. No one wished to live closer to Mystwood than they had to—no one, it seemed, except the estate's master.

The girl stopped and brought her hands up to her face, breathing on her fingers. Dressed in too-short pants, oversized boots that stayed up only thanks to old gray stockings, and a threadbare cream tunic that tried and failed to conceal her curves, she had to be freezing in the cool wind. It made River simultaneously want to envelop the girl in his arms and disembowel her overseer. Neither of which would be happening.

"That is female," Tye said after a moment.

"That is mortal," Coal added.

"That is a mistake," River declared with a finality he did not feel. If the girl was a mistake, his entire being wanted to be beside her anyway. His bones tingled with the pull of it even as he straightened to his full height, his voice a mix of command and dismissive closure. "One we must correct as expeditiously as possible."

"I don't think you fully appreciate how females work," said Tye dryly. From the Blaze Court, the southern most of the three fae kingdoms, Tye had thick red hair, a fire-magic affinity, and a propensity for finding a brothel anywhere, anytime—even if one hadn't existed there before Tye's arrival. He shifted his shoulders, his eyes locked on the girl. "They don't morph into males—let alone *fae* males—just because you order them to."

"You appreciate how females *work* enough for the rest of us put together, Tye." Coal crossed his arms, a stray lock of hair that had escaped his tight bun whipping in the fresh breeze. The warrior's face was tight, and River well understood Coal's displeasure. After a decade of seeking a fifth warrior to replace their fallen quint brother, the magic apparently had decided to play a damn jest and bond them with an utterly incompatible being. Quints were fae warrior units, magically chosen, eternally bonded, and harshly trained at the neutral Citadel Court to defend against the threats forever escaping from Mors, the dark realm. "She doesn't even feel us."

Coal's words twisted in River's chest. Yes, the male was correct. Any bonded fae warrior would be roaring his way toward the quint, unable to resist the pull, even if it meant striding right into Mystwood. The girl, on the other hand, was still shoveling manure.

"What now?" Coal asked, and it was all River could do not to flinch.

"We bring the mortal to the Citadel in Lunos and ask the Elders Council to break the bond." River turned his back on the girl whose essence now called to him. "Don't get attached."

LERALYNN

"*L*era!" Mimi's voice bounces through the stable, turning horses' heads.

"Over here," I call from the backmost stall, running my hand down a gelding's velvety neck. The horse whickers softly, his warm sides heaving as steam rises from his coat to mix with the stable's chill air. The earthy scent of hay and leather, tangled with the grassy waft of horse manure, wraps the stable in a familiarity that has become my refuge from Master Zake's mix of leers and blows.

Leaning my forehead against the horse, I draw long, steadying breaths. I'm on edge, have been since last night, though I can't put my finger on what's making my soul churn. Maybe it's the way Zake has been watching me lately, like I'm water in a drought—that should either be drunk up before it's gone or else sold for a tidy sum. Or maybe it's just the wolf from my dream that's still frightening me. Gray with black around the muzzle, golden eyes, and a powerful maw of sharp teeth. A foolish thing to be uneasy about. The only forest near

Zake's estate is Mystwood, which separates mortal lands from the fae. If there is a wolf in Mystwood, he wouldn't venture out. Animals don't like going in and out of those woods. And I don't blame them. I feel a shiver anytime I go near the forest's edge.

Actually, no one but Zake likes Mystwood, and he doesn't so much like the forest as worship it. Someone long ago told him that a clan of fae warriors shall one day emerge from the forest and take a human with them to the immortal lands. Zake filled in the rest of the tale with images of heroic battles, fawning women, and sparkling immortality. Thinking this too great a temptation to resist, the man built himself an estate at Mystwood's edge and has spent two decades waiting for fortune to show up with an invitation.

Perhaps I am too hard on the man, though—we all need something to dream about. Then again, mortals who try to cross into fae lands never return, though their bones and ravaged bodies sometimes appear at Mystwood's edge. Not all dreams are safe.

"Oh, bloody stars." Mimi puts her hands on her waist and regards me critically. "Get out of there before Zake gives you a new set of bruises. He pays you to mulch shit, not hug livestock."

"Zake pays me?" I say, raising a brow. I might theoretically be earning wages, but after Zake skims off my room and board and other "upkeep," as the indentured-servant trade calls it, I see little more than pennies.

Mimi grabs my wrist and hauls me out of the stall. She is even shorter than I am, the age my mother might be if she were still alive, and she works in the kitchens, so there is often a piece of bread or cheese in a pocket for me, together with a smell of flour trailing in her wake. Mimi is as close to family as

I've had since Zake purchased me from one of the orphan collectors twelve years ago. I don't remember what happened before then, but I do remember freezing one moment and being hauled atop a warm horse the next.

That was the one and only time I've ridden. I think Zake fears that I'll run off in the middle of the night if I could ride, though there is no place for me to go.

"Zake will give you a great deal more than pennies if you let him." Mimi brushes stray hay off my mane of auburn hair and arranges the locks over my shoulder. "He's been waiting for you for years, Leralynn, and I don't think he'll put up with your coyness for too much longer."

"If last week's whipping was a sign of courtship, I think he might be barking up the wrong tree. Never mind that he is twice my age and in love with a fairy tale."

Mimi clicks her tongue. "You might be the one in love with fairy tales, dear. Zake is *only* twice your age, is rough for work, not drink, and he's never once forced himself on you. How many masters would respect a stable girl's maidenhead, eh?"

"All the ones who think said maidenhead might fetch them a hefty sum."

Taking a warm roll from her pocket, Mimi stuffs it into mine, the smell of yeast and fresh bread making me groan. "I, for one, would enjoy calling you 'mistress.' You would live in the house, have food and clothing and heat. It would be a better life for you than cleaning stalls."

"I like cleaning stalls." Reaching back, I close the gelding's door, which slides smoothly on oiled wheels. Zake does take good care of his property—when he thinks it will line his pockets.

"Now, then." Mimi claps her hands. "Pay attention, girl. The kitchens are abuzz with rumors of a wolf stalking the

7

estate grounds. Master Zake's on his way back here to go hunting, and I thought it might be nice if you had a horse ready for him when he comes. Tell him to stay safe, fuss a bit. It wouldn't hurt."

I freeze, my mouth going dry. "Wolf?" I lick my lips. "What kind of wolf, Mimi?"

"I don't know. The meat-eating kind, I presume." She sighs. "You are focusing on the wrong part of the news. If you aren't going to be useful, then perhaps scram before Zake comes, eh? You don't need to be rejecting the man outright. And you might change your mind too."

Yes. Leave before Zake arrives heated for a hunt. That's exactly what I need to be doing.

Except I can't. I need to save that wolf. And I have no idea why.

"I can't scram—the horses want their dinner," I say mildly, as if my heart isn't galloping. "What has the wolf done?"

"Nothing yet." Mimi waves a hand dismissively. "With stars' fortune, Zake's men can put it down before it causes trouble and brings pack mates to help."

Pack mates. Yes, the wolf likely has those who'll mourn him and howl at the moon in loneliness, which I know too well. All because the innocent animal crossed Zake's property line.

The sounds of men's voices and clanging weapons ring from outside the barn door, and Mimi's face tightens. Unlike me, Mimi does what she is told and has almost saved enough to pay off her upkeep debts. "Come, girl. Either support the man or disappear from sight, eh?"

"You go." I push Mimi out the back stable entrance just as Master Zake pulls open the sliding front door. By the time his heavy boots echo through the stalls, I'm standing in the middle

of the aisle again, my thick locks billowing in the sudden gush
of wind.

The icy cold cuts my skin, making even my freckles shiver,
but I tighten my hold on the hay-filled wheelbarrow and
curtsy. "My lord."

Around forty, Zake is large, healthy, and muscular, with a
thick head of wiry brown hair. He's amassed a series of scars
to go along with his sharp temper, including a long slash across
his face that gives him a perpetually displeased expression.
Frowning at my wheelbarrow, Zake lifts a heavy saddle with
one hand and carries it into a stall. "You should have finished
with that half an hour ago, Leralynn," he calls. "Once I return
with this damn wolf's pelt, you and I shall discuss the meaning
of punctuality."

Bile rises in my throat. "Don't. Please, Master Zake."

Zake sticks his head out of the stall, his gaze raking my
body and making his scar stretch. "Don't whip you for
laziness?" he inquires with more interest than the question
warrants.

I hug my arms over my chest. "Don't hunt the wolf.
It . . . it might be a female." It isn't. But I don't know how I
know this, or what else to say. All I know, deep inside me, is
that hurting that wolf would be very, very bad. "Maybe she
has cubs. Little ones who nurse from her and need
her and—"

"Shade is most definitely not nursing cubs." The
unfamiliar voice, rich and musical, comes from the open stable
door. Where there was only wind moments ago, now I see a
tall man with deeply carved muscles, red hair, and amused
emerald-green eyes. Dressed in supple brown leather armor
that bares his long, corded arms, he moves with a feline grace
that should be impossible to achieve. His mouth, which seems

to be caught in a permanent smile, flashes white teeth with just a hint of point on the canines.

I've never seen something so beautiful.

He cocks his head at me and my breath catches.

Ears. Delicately pointed ears, one of which is crowned with an intricately worked silver earring. The man isn't a man at all, but an immortal fae male from beyond the Mystwood forest.

Zake seems to realize the same thing just as I do, and he gasps, eyes wide. Stepping in front of me, my master bows low to the visitor. "Welcome, High One." Zake's voice shakes a bit. "I've been awaiting you."

The man—the male—snorts, his eyes skipping over Zake to focus on mine. The nagging feeling inside my core pulses in recognition, but my mind remains blank. I have no idea who this male is, though my body seems to know him. I take a step back, my hand closing around a pitchfork.

The male's eyes glitter with amusement. "A pleasure to meet you as well, Lera," he drawls, his voice pulsing with a cockiness that I've a sudden desire to knock out of him. I know I should probably be terrified of the male, but instead I'm thinking that, if not for his ears and ethereal beauty, I'd imagine him just a few years older than I am, with his maturity perhaps lagging behind his body's dominating strength. Gaze firmly on my pitchfork, the male steps neatly around Zake and bows. "I'm Tye. And if it's an option, lass, I would prefer not to be skewered."

2

LERALYNN

"*P*lease forgive my servant's impudence, my lord," Zake says quickly, bowing as he steps between me and the fae warrior again. Zake's voice drips with desire, like a salivating dog. "It is but a misunderstanding. It is I, not this wench, who's waited for you here at Mystwood's edge. I will of course fulfil the honorable request you make of my estate."

Tye gives Zake a dismissive look and raises a bemused eyebrow at me, as if to say, *Who the hell is this?*

"Excuse us." Grabbing my arm, Zake pulls me out the back door of the stable, his large fingers leaving bruises above my elbow. The cold pierces me from all sides, cutting brutally through my thin clothes, but my blood is racing too quickly to worry about the chill. Zake's nostrils flare, a vein ticking along his temple. "What the hell is this?" he hisses into my face, his rank breath shoving itself inside me. "You think to steal my destiny from under my very nose?"

I try and fail to wrench my arm from his grasp. "I'm not

stealing anything." My breath mists, the words coming quickly as I spot his free hand unbuckling his heavy belt. "I've not even laid eyes on a fae male before now, Zake. I swear it on the bloody stars."

"Is this why you tried to stop my hunt?" Zake snarls into my face. "You wanted to intercept the immortal before he reached me?" His meaty hand turns me around, pressing my head against the barn's side as the belt uncoils behind me. "What did you offer him, wench? Your maidenhead? Tell me the truth now, girl—it will only hurt more if you lie."

"I'm not lying," I say, my body already bracing for the coming blows. "Zake—" I clamp my mouth shut as the belt whistles through the air. There is no stopping this now, and little reason to waste breath that I'll need shortly.

A furious growl rips through the air. Just when my back is supposed to explode in flame, a dark shape hurtles out of nowhere. Before I can blink, Zake is in the dirt, a large wolf prowling over him. The wolf's lips pull back, revealing wet canines that glitter in the sun, its thick gray pelt and black muzzle bringing me straight back to last night's dream.

I gasp, stepping away—and knock right into a wall of muscle and maleness. Tye, the smiling red-haired fae male, is no longer amused. The green-eyed stare he gives Zake is filled with the promise of violence. Not that there will be much of Zake left if the wolf has his way.

"What's going on back here?" says a quiet voice. A new fae male strides out of the stable, this one dressed in warrior black and sporting a glare that says he's one breath away from razing the whole estate to the ground. If Tye is an overgrown adolescent, the newcomer is a deadly killer, with long blond hair tied up in a bun, a chiseled jaw, and piercing blue eyes that seem to strip me and find me wanting in one glance. The wicked-looking blades strapped to his waist and back complete the effect.

"Just a wee misunderstanding," says Tye. "I have it handled."

The warrior snorts. "That'd be a first."

Tye sighs in a long-suffering way. "Lera, this is Coal. Try to ignore him the best you can."

Coal crosses his arms, his eyes finishing their examination of the soon-to-be-dead Zake and the salivating wolf before coming to a stop on my face.

As with Tye, a ripple of recognition races through me, though I'm certain I've never seen this male before. My instincts scream at me to run, even as the male's eyes draw me toward him, the corded muscles of his forearms and shoulders making my breath quicken.

"Time to go, lass," Tye murmurs into the back of my neck. A command. An invitation. A challenge.

Murderous fae. Mystwood. Broken bones.

My heart pounds, even as my body feels the rightness of Tye's words and aches to accept them. I swallow, feeling as though the male has claimed me already. And not just him. *Five,* my soul seems to whisper.

Five what?

Five. There should be five. Has to be five.

Still pinned to the ground, Zake whimpers, his hoarse voice forcing itself between the males and me. "Call off your beast. Please. You can have the wench if you want her. A present. A goodwill—"

"Enough games." Coal pulls out his sword, the steel sighing against the sheath. "I'm putting it down."

He doesn't mean the wolf.

I shudder. "Don't." My words are a hopeless whisper, but both males and even the wolf snap their heads to me at once, their eyes questioning. As if what I say matters—what I want matters. I take a tentative breath, wondering how far this input of mine will carry. "Zake doesn't deserve to die."

"Yes, he does," says Coal, his words ice. The wolf growls his agreement.

"He does," Tye says behind me. "But it is your choice to make, lass. We will not touch him if you wish it so."

My heart pounds against my chest, bruising my ribs. This morning I'd had a say in exactly nothing, and now these immortals, these fae males who could raze or rule the entire mortal world if they wanted to, are placing Zake's life in my hands. They want to hurt him. But they won't. For me. "Let him go." My voice is thin, as if trying to hide itself in case this evening is one big jest. "Please."

Coal scowls at Zake but sheaths his blade. Tye's warm breath shudders against my neck. The wolf is the last to obey, snapping his teeth inches from Zake's eyes before stepping off the prone man, lifting his leg, and urinating.

I clamp my hand over my mouth to bite back a very inappropriate chuckle.

"So you do have a sense of humor," Tye says approvingly from behind me, wrapping his cloak around my shoulder. I don't know what the cloak is made of, but it is the warmest thing I've ever worn, with thick green woolen cloth and a fur lining that caresses my skin. The smell of pine and citrus fills my nose, matching the scent of the male behind me.

"Get out of here, traitor," Zake roars at me from the ground. "I always knew you were nothing but a cursed wench, a common wh—"

The wolf leans over him again with a fierce growl and Zake shuts his mouth, but there is no unsaying the words.

I can no longer stay at Zake's estate, and there is no place for me to go but wherever these immortals take me.

3

TYE

*L*era's hand clamped over her mouth, stifling a chuckle as Shade's piss soaked the piece of excrement calling itself Zake. Her laughter's soft vibration echoed through Tye's body, and for the first time since Lera's hand had tightened on the pitchfork, Tye felt hope stir in his chest. She might come with them. This ferocious, brave, fragile, beautiful woman might come with them to Lunos. With quint-called fae, there was never a question—once the magic chose its prey, there was no physical resistance one could offer against the need to bond with the quint. But magic seemed to work differently on the mortal lass.

Lera could say no.

And Tye's heart raced like the wind in terror of that one word. Which was not something the others needed to know. He made himself grin. "So you do have a sense of humor."

Shade finished urinating and used his back paws to toss a bit of dirt onto the wet form. Zake truly deserved worse, but

Tye and his quint brothers would stand by Lera's word. This was her territory, her conflict, her decision.

Unclasping his cloak, Tye eased the rich green fabric from his back and wrapped it around Lera's slender shoulders, ignoring Coal's hard glare. Tye was *not* marking the female with his scent—the lass was ice cold and it chafed Tye to see her so. Coal might consider freezing to be a character-building exercise, but other sentient beings could certainly disagree.

Plus, whether Lera accepted the cloak or not was likewise her choice.

Tye hid a smile as Lera pulled the fabric around herself, inhaling deeply. Her body softened, the tension in her shoulders easing. Tye's nostrils flared, savoring the subtle scent of her pleasure. Her other, more dominant scents were already familiar to him. Sweet hay and lilac flower, tinged with something fresh and rich, like ripe berries. Lera's hair, a warm reddish brown, fell away to expose her neck, which throbbed with her rapid heartbeat. Tye's cock twitched, his mouth longing to press over the female's trembling pulse.

"Get out of here, traitor," the trash on the ground roared, disgustingly oblivious to just how close he was to being put down. "I always knew you were nothing but a cursed wench, a common wh—"

Shade growled. Shade's wolf was intelligent, but with saturated instincts, he could strike first and fret over it later. Fortunately, Zake proved wise enough to shut up and Coal was already moving to place himself between Shade and the miserable human.

Which left Tye and Lera. "Come, lass," Tye said softly into her ear as he stepped around to where she could see his face, his skin still tingling from when she'd leaned lightly into him. "River is waiting with the horses."

"How many of you are there?" Lera asked, looking at Coal. At bloody Coal! Which was just humiliating.

Tye scowled.

"Four," Coal said brusquely.

Tye held out his hand, reclaiming Lera's attention. "Five, including you. If we could get moving before River grows cranky, it would be good."

Lera didn't move, but she didn't step away either. Tye could smell her blood's rapid racing. Of course it was racing. A pack of bloody immortals had just descended upon her life, got her evicted, and were now intending to whisk her away to a place where mortals were not welcome. If not for Zake, Shade, and Coal, Tye would have had an easier time calming the lass.

He stepped toward her slowly, making sure Lera could see each of his movements as he hooked an arm under her knees and lifted her easily against his chest.

The lass's eyes widened.

"Your legs are short," Tye declared, adjusting her to fit perfectly against his shoulder as he strode to where River was already mounted, Coal and Shade trailing behind them. "It's faster this way than waiting for you to walk."

Lera's eyes narrowed at him. "I've been walking just fine for twenty years."

"Good to know." Tye gave her a cocky grin. "Look, that's the one and only River you asked about. He's the quint commander, and if you think you see a stick so far up his arse that it's coming out his nose, then you are right."

River's gray eyes glared down at Tye. Sitting atop his stallion, the male wore a tailored dark-blue coat, black trousers, and mirror-shined black boots. His hair, dark brown and cropped close to his head, accentuated his strong back and shoulders as he held two more large stallions by the reins. Yes, River wore an air of command like a cloak—and as far as Tye was concerned, he was welcome to it.

"Hurry up." River shifted his gaze to the road in front of them, as if he were already halfway down it in his mind, meeting and addressing obstacles that had yet to enter Tye's imagination. "The mortal rides with Coal."

"Like hell she does." Tye's shoulders tightened and he glared at River, even as he pulled Lera closer to him. The lass had just let Tye handle her, and he wasn't about to let the moment end so soon. "We—"

"She rides with Coal," River repeated, turning finally to show his canines. Their commander rarely pulled rank like this, so it carried an annoying amount of weight when he did. River could be an utter bastard sometimes.

"Yes, *sir*," said Tye. The only sign that River heard his tone was a slight tick in his jaw.

Tye gave Coal a warning look before handing the lass up to him, and he swallowed a bit of ill-placed jealousy when the warrior tucked Lera neatly before him in the saddle, bracing his arms securely on either side of her waist as he took up the reins again. At least Coal would not let her fall. That was the important part.

Tye dropped back to fall in line beside River. "What the hell was that about?" he demanded, his voice too low for Lera to hear. "Or are you planning to issue orders for everything now? If so, I'd like your permission to take a shit in approximately two hours."

River snorted. "Don't pretend you failed to notice that our fifth is female." He gave Tye a hard look. "You've not walked past a female without stopping for a chat in the three centuries I've known you."

"You've not stopped to talk to one in just as long," said Tye. "Someone needs to keep this quint—"

River's hand shot out to grip Tye's wrist. Hard. "Not. Her. She is a mortal, Tye, a female mortal. The magic's call to her was a mistake. Our priority is to break the bond before it gets her killed. Understand?"

"I'm not going to rut with her, River." Tye twisted his hand from River's grip. "But you've no call to be an asshole to her either. Lera is one of us now. One of the quint. Don't tell me you don't feel it, that your soul doesn't twist when she comes close."

River's nostrils flared. "It doesn't."

"Liar."

"It isn't real," River forced out finally, his jaw tightening. The horse beneath him danced, sensing his agitation. River sighed and patted the horse's neck until the animal calmed down. "The feeling . . . the need, it's nothing but the work of magic. The mortal is nothing to me, nothing to us. Once the magic is severed—"

"Not real?" Tye said harshly. "These feelings are born of the same magic that shattered us after Kai's loss. Or is that *not real* as well?" It was a low blow, even for Tye.

River's fist flew at Tye's jaw, but Tye didn't bother blocking the assault. It pissed River off royally when someone failed to defend himself, and right now River deserved a bit of misery. Maybe it would force the male's head from his ass, though that might be too optimistic an outlook.

River blamed himself for the death of Shade's twin, for the pain that made Shade retreat into his wolf for a decade now. None of them could lift their heads after it happened, but Tye thought River and Shade had suffered the most. It was hard to tell with Coal, who buried everything so deep you'd need to

21

slice him open just to find a feeling. The quint were brothers in all but blood, and they'd spilled enough of that together that it was likely mixed by now too.

Lifting his chin, Tye let the blood from his newly split lip dribble onto his chin. "Feeling better?"

"It *is* just the magic, Tye," River said stubbornly, kicking his horse into a gallop. "Once the bond is severed, releasing her will not affect you . . . us . . . the same way. It will not be like losing Kai all over again."

No, losing Lera would not be like losing Kai, Tye thought. It would be worse.

4

COAL

*C*oal was going to kill River, he decided, as Leralynn squirmed in his saddle, her flesh pressing against Coal's and setting every nerve in his body aflame. The mortal had been in his charge for less than a minute and already her sweet hay-and-lilac scent was making his head spin. Tye might have savored being in Coal's skin just now, but Coal was different from his quint brothers.

Tye enjoyed women like he enjoyed exquisite desserts, sampling freely without commitment, leaving all involved with a pleasant—if fleeting—aftertaste. River, who still mourned the female he'd loved before the quint call took him, kept his distance. The quint commander never lacked for invitations, but he rarely if ever took a female to his bed. Shade, who once shared females with his twin Kai, had retreated into his wolf a decade back, unwilling to touch a female without his twin alongside.

As for Coal, he was unfit for female company. Too many jagged edges, too deep a darkness. Three hundred years had passed since the quint call rescued him, but time didn't erase the past.

What Coal needed just now was some wind, a bit of fresh air to clear the girl's scent from his nose. The mortal realm dampened the fae's magic, but there were old-fashioned ways of calling the wind to your face. Coal patted his horse's flank once and nudged the stallion into a canter.

Leralynn gasped, bouncing so hard in the saddle that the horse bucked in bewilderment. The girl's fingernails dug into Coal's forearms as if the whole bloody world was falling on their ears, and she slid further sideways than Coal thought possible given their arrangement. Coal cursed, hauling his nearly-unsaddled-for-no-reason passenger back into place and holding fast with his arms tucked even tighter against her waist as she attempted to topple off again.

The horse whinnied unhappily.

"You don't know how to ride, mortal." He'd meant it as a question, but it sounded more like a murder accusation.

"The mortal's name is Lera," she snapped over her shoulder, grabbing on to the horse's neck and wiggling. "And we are not all immortal fae who own horses. Have you not met someone who couldn't ride before?"

"Not in over three hundred years, no." Coal turned his head and took a deep breath of fresh air. Leralynn's—Lera's—shifting backside happened to be very well aligned with his cock. With another curse—this one swallowed before he voiced it—Coal hurried to tighten his arms around the girl before her attempts to find purchase in the saddle awoke him any further.

"Three hundred years? You are over three—" Lera's voice hitched. "Feel free to explain what's happening anytime now. Where we are going would be a nice start. What under the bloody stars is happening would also be a welcome topic."

"We will find camp for the night, then cross Mystwood to enter Lunos, then ride to the Citadel to ask the Elders Council to break your bond with our quint," Coal said, his words clipped. The female was starting to lean into him now, her body tentatively trusting his to keep her safe. It was bloody intoxicating, the warmth and need that Lera's closeness sent through his flesh. No, not the mortal's closeness—just the magic that had accidentally, and very temporarily, bonded them together. Gritting his teeth, Coal made his hips still, refusing to let his body sink deeper into hers—even as his every fiber fought to rearrange itself to fit tighter around Lera's curves. Coal *would* keep her safe. From falling, from attack, from himself.

"That isn't an explanation," said Lera. "That's a recitation of facts that you know perfectly well I don't understand." Her voice was musical and strong, but Coal could smell the biting tendrils of fear beneath the bravado. Fear that a promise of not falling from a horse wouldn't soothe.

He'd been afraid too when the quint call came. Terrified. Not of dying, but of living, of being recaptured and brought back to his masters in chains. "Do you know what Mors is?" he asked.

She shook her head, her whole body shifting along with it and waking Coal again.

He ground his teeth. He'd need to start with the basics. "Mors is the dark realm, where beings called qoru live. They are gray-skinned creatures who ingest others' life energy to survive, the same as how fae and humans require food. Qoru raised harvests of fae and humans as a food source and to work for them." Releasing the reins with one hand, Coal

25

traced a line across Lera's forearm, close to her wrist. She shivered lightly and he felt it all the way to his toes. "Several thousand years ago, a host of fae and humans escaped Mors, establishing the fae lands, which we call Lunos." He traced a second line, this one a bit closer to the elbow. "The fae built up the wards to keep the wall between Mors and Lunos erect. While Lunos was mostly safe from Mors's nightmares, the inequality between the immortal, magically gifted fae and their weaker but more numerous human counterparts created its own problems. So the humans moved on," Coal traced a third line, this one across the crook of Lera's elbow, "creating the mortal lands and helping set up Mystwood to ensure that the worlds remain separate."

"You said *mostly* safe," said Lera, and Coal's brow twitched. Sharp attention on this one.

"Just as Mystwood is not wholly impermeable to passage, the wall between Mors and Lunos likewise has weaknesses. Occasionally, things pass that should not." Coal's body tensed, this time without Lera's movement. He cleared his throat. "As Lunos settled into itself, three courts emerged— Flurry, the Ice Court in the north; Slait, the Earth Court in the middle; and Blaze, the Fire Court in the south. With three courts, each concerned for itself, Lunos became fragmented against Mors's threat. The elders of each court thus combined their powers to form the Citadel, a neutral fortress charged with protecting Lunos. The Citadel's magic calls fae in troupes of five, the bond making the quint's power greater than any fae warrior alone." Coal paused, making sure she was listening closely. He felt her attention in the stiffness of her back, her hands clinging tightly to his arms. "River, Tye, Shade, and I are one such quint. We lost our fifth quint brother ten years ago and have waited for the magic to choose another to complete us. It appears that the magic has chosen you."

"To join your . . . quint?" said Lera.

"Yes."

"Of deadly immortal warriors."

"Yes."

Coal didn't know what exactly he expected next—panic, a stream of babbling questions, crying—but it wasn't this calm silence. The mortal seemed to be considering, thinking. Plotting all their deaths, if she was smart.

This silence, broken only by the soft beat of the horses' hooves and the occasional equine snort, was not kind to Coal's body, making him all too aware of the female's presence. Her softness pressing into his pelvis and stomach, her thighs lining the inside of his. Her scent, which somehow bypassed his nose and went directly to his cock. Yes, Coal was going to kill River for this.

"This Citadel," Lera said finally, halting Coal's thoughts with a violent jerk. "How does it work?"

"The Citadel trains, tests, and commands the quints. That is where we head now. The Elders Council will be able to sever this mistaken bond and set you free of us."

He'd meant that last part to be soothing, but the female's body remained tense, as if she didn't dare believe him. "Do fae apply to the Citadel?" she asked finally. "Is there some kind of selection process?"

"No. The original elders set up the magic to select the warriors. It keeps the Citadel neutral and prevents any court from planting its allies in the quints. For the fae, once the call comes, there is no physical choice but to answer it. The magic always calls beings from different courts into one bond; that, too, the elders made by design. Most of the quints are male, though a few female ones exist. There are no mixed-gender quints, save the Elders Council itself."

"The Elders Council and us, you mean," the mortal said.

"No. He means only the Elders Council," River's voice interrupted, the commander pulling his horse up beside Coal's and narrowing his eyes at them both. "We aren't a quint—we are a mistake. There can't be a human in a fae warrior bond."

Lera flinched and Coal's arms tightened around her reflexively. The fact that River was right didn't make Coal want to punch the male any less. That was the luxury of not being in charge, of not being the one to carry responsibility for the whole quint and more—you could be as pissed as you wanted at the one who made the calls. Coal bowed in his saddle and veered far enough away to let Lera breathe again.

That proved to be its own mistake. The moment her heart slowed, the mortal started talking again. "Where are you all from?"

Coal's jaw flexed. He should have just kept his mouth shut, but it was too late now. "River is from Slait. Tye is from Blaze. Shade and his twin Kai were from Flurry."

"And you?" Lera gasped as they headed down a hill and the stallion's gait became choppy. The saddle was chafing the inside of the female's knees and thighs, the copper scent of her increasingly bloody wounds making Coal's heart pound. She wasn't complaining, though, even if her questions came through gritted teeth. "Which court are you from?"

Instead of answering, Coal kicked the stallion into a gallop. The sooner they got to camp and moved the female off horseback, the better.

5

LERALYNN

$\mathscr{J}$ swallow a scream as Coal sends our horse into a gallop, his patience with answering my questions plainly exhausted. The horse's powerful muscles flex and extend under me, the chill wind making my eyes water. After years of wishing to ride these magnificent beasts, the reality is crushing. Rolling pastures race by in streaks of yellow and green, while Mystwood's forbidding gloom gets ever closer. The saddle chafes my legs raw, and my body, which rises a bit into the air and lands hard with each mighty thump of the horse's hooves, is pounding with pain. I'd be tossed to a certain death if not for the hard arms bracing my waist in cold silence.

A parasite, that's what I am to him. An unwanted growth attached by a magical mishap. The males might be civil enough now, but that will change once they, like Coal, realize how pathetic I am beside them, how little I know of things they take for granted. Like sitting atop a moving animal without breaking my neck.

River's words grind like sand into my flesh, working

themselves deeper with each of the stallion's strides. I'm a mistake of magic, a set of shackles clamped onto four immortal beings.

After an hour of freezing pounding, my endurance reaches its limit and I let the tears welling in my eyes spill onto my cheeks, my shoulders trembling from cold and pain. I try to hold it in, but I can't stop the wet gasps as each jolt opens the skin on my thighs further.

A soft growl escapes Coal's mouth. Without slowing the horse, the male spares one arm from the reins to clamp around my abdomen like an iron band, which keeps me from bouncing about. Within a minute, he is clicking his tongue and urging his horse into an even faster gallop, as if determined to outrun the setting sun.

Shutting my eyes, I bury my hands in Coal's forearm, feeling his muscles tense and relax with each jolting step. I try to breathe deeply, to inhale his scent of leather and salt, and imagine a bard's tale for myself. In my tale, I'm not a prisoner on horseback but the one urging the beast into a run, while the strong arms keeping me in the saddle are a lover's embrace instead of a tether to counteract my incompetence. In my tale, these males who make my chest tighten are not trying to get rid of me.

"Tye." Coal's voice cuts through the icy air and I realize that we've stopped moving. The horse's flanks heave, and steam rises from his sweaty coat. "Get over here and take the mortal."

I blink at what looks like a small inn of rough stone. A smoking chimney and a fire glimmering through the common room's windows promise blissful warmth. My stomach growls and I realize I've not eaten in some time, the once-warm roll Mimi stuffed into my pocket now squished into crumbs—

though possibly still salvageable. The thought of Mimi makes my heart clench. I never said goodbye to her before leaving. Though given her hopes for Zake and me, I think she'd have called me a fool. And she would have been right.

"What the bloody hell are we doing here?" Tye asks mildly as Coal hands me down to him. I fall gracelessly into the male's arms, my feet on the ground but my shaking legs unable to support my full weight. "Not that I mind an inn with fair maids, but River may have a comment or two."

"River certainly does," says River, pulling up beside us. "We've brought enough attention to ourselves as it is."

"Desire and reality aren't melding for you tonight," Coal tells River curtly. "We can go no farther today."

Tye's nostrils flare delicately above my neck. As if . . .

"Are you sniffing me?" I ask, craning my neck to look at the green-eyed male.

Instead of answering, Tye slips a hand beneath my knees and lifts me off the ground, cradling me against his chest as he starts toward the inn door. "Coal is right, we need to stay here tonight," he calls over his shoulder. "For the record, the lass was whole when I handed her off to that bastard."

I squirm in Tye's grip. "Let me down. Where do you imagine I'll run off to?"

"You'll fall, Lilac Girl," Tye purrs, ignoring my struggles while River demands rooms from a wide-eyed innkeeper. Even without the pointed ears and the wolf trotting beside the horses, my quint males would never blend with human men. From fierce-eyed Coal to towering River, they are too tall, too chiseled, too beautiful to be anything but immortal.

The innkeeper bows low, rubbing his wrist. "I would most love to oblige you, my lord, but you see, we are all sold out. Not one room—"

"Then become vacant," River says in a voice that sends a shudder down my spine, each violent story of the fae vivid in my mind.

Blood drains from the innkeeper's face, and he bows so low he trips over his own feet. "Of course. I'll . . . I'll shift some guests. They can double up in beds with no trouble, I'm certain. Please, my lords, follow me. It's an honor to have you here."

Tye snorts softly and tightens his hold on me as he carries me further inside, leaving River and the sounds of coin changing hands behind us. River is paying, it appears, and very handsomely.

I wonder how I'm going to repay whatever the males are spending for my upkeep, but I can't bring myself to protest. My body needs sustenance and a place to sleep too desperately to consider the costs. Tye follows a serving girl up a wobbly wooden staircase and into a large room with a plush green featherbed, a small dresser with a washbasin, and a wide leather armchair tucked into the corner.

"You aren't our prisoner, you know," Tye whispers into my ear, sending a shiver all the way through me. His perfect face hovers inches away from mine, the heat from his cheek seeping through my skin and teasing my flesh. Dismissing the servant with a flick of his hair, Tye lowers me gently onto the bed.

The down mattress sinks luxuriously under my weight, hugging my sore body. I fail to contain a small moan before blinking myself back to reality.

Bed. I am on a bed with a fae male who technically kidnapped me and is now so close that I could bathe in his pine-and-citrus scent. Tye's red hair flops over his eyes, and my fingers long to brush it away, to tuck it behind that exquisitely pointed ear of his. I wrap my arms around myself. "So I'm free to leave whenever I wish?"

Tye's normally sunny face tightens and he retreats from me, his triceps flexing as he rises. He perches on the far corner of the bed. Even then, he is so large that the mattress shifts beneath his weight. "Is that what you would like, lass?" Tye asks, his voice even.

"It little matters what I'd like, does it?" I snap, fatigue taking the reins of my tongue. A parasite. A set of shackles. A mistake. "Coal explained the basics to me. I'm stuck with you four until the Citadel elders sever the bond, thus freeing the magic to choose someone else for you. Someone more male and immortal than I am." Someone who can contribute. "The faster we can make that happen, the better. Am I right?"

Tye studies the floor for a long moment before shaking himself and rising to his feet. "You are. I'll see about some food and a bath being sent to your room." The male offers me a slight bow and strides out the door without looking back, leaving me with an emptiness that has no business blossoming in my chest.

The food arrives, as promised—a mouthwatering beef stew, thick with carrots, potatoes, and onions. The heel of bread beside my bowl is thick and soft. I'm using the last bit of crust to mop up the remains of the delicious broth when servants appear with a tub, buckets of steaming water, and a set of clothing. They give me as wide a berth as the room allows, casting glances that range from pity to fear when they think I'm not looking.

Drawing my legs up to my chest, I push myself into the corner of the bed. My body is one large bruise, and with the males gone, a chilling emptiness settles around my shoulders. Pulling Tye's cloak closer to my face, I take a deep whiff, the lingering pine-and-citrus scent calming my nerves until the servants leave and the steam from the tub tickles the air.

Right. Laying Tye's cloak carefully on the bed, I strip off the rest of my clothing and sink into the blissfully hot water. Someone added drops of lilac oil to the water and left a cake of lavender soap on a thick towel beside the tub. It's many times more than a lifelong servant like me deserves, but there is nothing to be gained by leaving the soap alone.

I've just finished working up the thickest lather I've ever seen when the door creaks open and soft feet tap against the floor. I sink beneath the soap bubbles, turning cautiously to find a pair of yellow eyes staring into mine.

The scream that starts deep in my chest spills into my mouth, and I clamp both hands over my lips to keep the sound in check. The last thing I want is the world running into my room to find me naked. As for the yellow-eyed wolf . . .

"Hello, Shade," I say to the giant predator prancing toward me, his tale high up in the air. Now that he isn't snarling over Zake's form, he looks more like a gray plush toy than a deadly killer of Mystwood. I've no notion as to whether he understands human speech, but I might as well be polite. "Would you mind closing the door?"

Shade cocks his head, flicks his right ear, and proceeds to sniff the base of the tub, then the room itself, and finally leaps smoothly onto my bed to curl up into a large ball of deadly fluff.

Grabbing the towel that the servants left for me, a thick woven terrycloth with just the right amount of softness, I wrap it around myself as I step out of the tub. My thick hair drips in darkened brown waves down my shoulders as I pad to the door and push it closed again. My back now to the wall, I assess the situation. Namely, the presence of a large sleeping wolf in the middle of the mattress that I'd fully intended on occupying.

"I'll share the bed," I tell Shade, "but you are not evicting me to sleep in a chair."

Shade's ear flickers but his eyes remain closed and his considerable bulk shows no signs of relocating.

Body still wrapped in a towel, I climb onto an unoccupied part of the bed and tentatively push Shade with my foot.

The wolf growls without opening his eyes. The rumbling sound echoes through my body, failing to insight fear. I know this wolf. Somewhere deep in my soul, if not my head.

"Fine." I curl myself into a ball and slip under the covers, a calm finally washing over me despite the invasion of my privacy and space. The room, still warm from the steam, sways as fatigue claims me. After a few heartbeats, the mattress shifts as Shade rises and circles in search of a better spot. When the wolf settles again, I feel his warm breath on the back of my neck and a solid mass of muscle and fur pressing against my curved spine.

"I dreamed about you, wolf," I murmur, my eyes closed. My hand reaches back, caressing the wolf's soft fur, and the beast purrs beneath my touch, the sound a rumble that vibrates his body. I smile. "Before I ever met you, I knew you."

6

LERALYNN

$\mathcal{I}$ wake, as I usually do, before the sun rises. Shade groans his discontent as I extricate myself from his warm body, but he tucks his nose under his tail and goes back to sleep quickly enough. Slipping into the clothes the servants brought for me last night—a long-sleeved green dress that brings out my eyes and a pair of warm stockings, which all fit wonderfully beneath Tye's cloak—I slide out of the room and make my way down the wobbly staircase. My mind spins with yesterday's news, and I've always done my best thinking while working.

The inn's small stable is right beside the main house, and the familiar scents of leather, hay, and horse greet me like old friends. Of the eight stalls, six are occupied with the males' stallions—the horses being so big as to require stall partitions to be temporarily lifted to create larger quarters. Finding a set of currycombs, brushes, and hoof picks on a dusty shelf, I bring Coal's horse out of his stall. The black stallion follows me with his ears forward and his nostrils flaring in excitement.

He reminds me of his master—proud, quietly strong, with more than a touch of untamed wildness under the surface. A preternatural beast that is too great and beautiful for this world.

"Sorry, boy—we're not actually going for a ride. Best I can offer is some grass while I brush you," I inform the horse, who is already pawing the ground. Bringing him outside, I let him graze on a patch of lush grass while I work the toothy currycomb through his glorious velvet coat.

I'm working on the horse's hooves when a stable lad of about ten appears, a heavy saddle balanced on his hip. "You'll be wanting his tack, then, mistress?" the boy says, eyeing the horse appreciatively.

I'm about to say no when a new thought strikes me. If I'm going to be riding with the fae, it would little hurt to get comfortable in the saddle. Given my body's protest at the mere thought of mounting the horse, I would rather conquer that bridge without an audience present. "Do you think you could help me?" I ask the boy. "I'd just like to ride him around the paddock here, but I could use a bit of instruction from a horseman like yourself."

The boy nods sagely, freckles shifting with his growing grin. "I'll fetch you a mounting block, mistress," he calls, racing to retrieve a small stepstool while I ease the saddle onto the horse's back and tighten the straps.

By the time the boy returns, I have the stallion saddled and bridled. The horse's excited whinny adds courage to my plan, especially when he walks eagerly to the mounting block and stands rock still as I haul my aching body into the saddle.

The next three heartbeats are the most glorious of my life. My head, spine, hips, and heels align together, the perfect power of the horse beneath me rising through my core. It's as if the whole might of the world has been condensed and made into a stallion and, through him, into me.

"Looking fine, mistress," the boy says approvingly, removing the mounting block. "Take up the reins now."

I reach for the leather. Sensing a shift of weight, the horse steps forward, the saddle moving beneath me. My heart quickens and I grab on to the pommel, my legs clamping around the stallion's sides to keep me in place. "Take up the reins," the boy calls, a hint of alarm entering his voice.

I snatch up the leather strips with due haste, pulling them tight to my body.

The stallion shakes his head angrily, pulling the rough leather right out of my fingers. I make a grab for my target again, this time holding fast against any further attitude. As my grip tightens on the reins, the horse brings his weight onto his hindquarters, throwing me against the tall back of the saddle. I yelp, my body tightening just as the stallion lurches forward with a speed to rival a storm. The stable boy shouts something I can't make out over the rushing wind and my own pounding heart.

Terror rips through me as the ground and trees race by in streaks of color and stone. My hands, still clutching the reins, claw into the horse's mane, my feet losing the stirrups as my rear rises and crashes. The stallion turns sharply and my stomach sinks as I lift off the saddle, crashing back onto it through sheer fortune.

My heart stutters.

Thud-ump, thud-ump, thud-ump, the horse's hooves pound, each step threatening to end my life. *Thud-ump, thud-ump, thud-ump.*

A branch hits my face and I look up to find Mystwood rising before me, its trees thick and foreboding. Animals hate those woods, and I breathe a sigh of relief that the stallion will slow and veer away rather than enter.

Instead, the horse's ears press flat against his head and he thunders directly into the thicket without slowing his step. Right—it's a bloody fae horse. It probably thinks it's heading home for bloody supper. *Thud-ump, thud-ump, thud-ump.* The world flashes before me—the stones that will turn the horse's legs, the tree trunks that come within a hair of slamming into my knees, the males who I may never see again. Another branch strikes my face, leaving a bloody gash across my cheek, as the horse gallops on along the winding path of Mystwood, the reins and my screams trailing in his wake.

These woods are nothing like any forest I've been in before, the moss-covered trees seeming to lean in as I approach them. The sun shines in some places, but others are as dark as night under many feet of green canopy.

Another sharp turn. Another miracle of survival. And then my fortune ends with a fallen tree blocking our path four feet off the ground.

I register the barrier, my eyes widening with the lack of options. There is no place to turn. Nowhere to go but up, up, up, higher than I can survive. My mouth opens in a wordless scream but the horse shows no sign of slowing. Five paces to go. Three. None. The horse braces his weight on his hindquarters and leaps into the air.

I fly off. The ground races up to meet me. The triumph of impact comes before the shocking echo of it, my shoulder screaming in pain as the world blinks in and out of darkness. I whimper, curling around my left arm, telling myself that I am alive.

I hear it then. A horrid, immortal sound, like the scrape of nails on a slate mixed with the lower notes of gurgling phlegm.

The woods crackle, branches snapping to my right. And left. And . . . the gurgling growl sounds again. More than one now. Closing in on me from many directions at once.

Whatever beast has found me in Mystwood, it did not come alone.

7

LERALYNN

*F*ight or run? My breath comes fast, the pain in my shoulder slowing to a distant, dull roar as I gather my legs under me. The gurgling growls are moving closer and I still don't know whether I'm better off trying to outrun it— them—or fight. Neither. I can do neither. Clean-picked bones. Mauled bodies. That is what's found of humans who try to cross Mystwood.

The branches shift, and despite the futility of it, my good hand tightens around a rock just as three . . . creatures step out around me.

I scream, the sound piercing Mystwood.

The things might charitably be called a mix of hog and human. They stand on hind legs, their front limbs long enough to run on all fours. The knees bend back like an animal's, and their faces . . . red vertical slits for eyes, a snout of a nose, a protruding lower jaw with fangs that stick out for apparent lack of room inside the maw. Their lips—if the flaps of skin covering their mouths can be called that—fail at blocking yellow saliva from dripping onto their fur-covered torsos.

The worst, though, is the delight flashing in those glowing eyes, which widen in concert with the increasing flow of saliva. They are not just going to kill me—they are going to savor every moment of it.

Fight *and* run. Launching the stone in my hand into the closest beast's snout, I scramble to my feet and sprint down the trail. One step. Two. Before my third stride lands, a massive weight crashes into me from behind. I fall onto my stomach, hot slime dripping onto the back of my neck and the stench of rotten meat so thick that I gag.

Claws dig deep into my flesh, the pain a hot flame. This is how I die, then. At the claws and jaws of a nightmare. I brace for the killing blow just as another roar echoes through the trees, this one familiar and furious.

Shade sprints toward us, a blur of gray fur and shining yellow eyes. Without slowing, the wolf lowers to the ground, his teeth snapping as he launches his body at the thing atop me. My breath stills. With the next beat of my heart, the weight on my back disappears, the rot replaced by a wolf's earthy scent. I struggle up, holding my arm close, and find Shade atop the hog beast that held me down moments ago. Blood the color of rust spills from the hog beast's mauled neck onto the forest floor, Shade's muzzle dripping with more of the viscous substance.

The other two hog beasts snarl their displeasure, circling Shade and me. They are twice the wolf's size and salivating again, unconcerned with the fate of their companion. One of the two takes a step forward, and Shade is between it and me in a moment. The wolf's sides heave, whether from the sprint here or the fight he's already had. Without the element of surprise, he cannot fight off both hog beasts at once.

I put my good hand on Shade's back. "Run, wolf. I can't run, but you can. Let's not have two deaths where there need be only one." I bite my lip and shove Shade away. "Go, wolf! Run, damn you."

My shoving fails to dislodge Shade but sends lightning up my injured shoulder. My escaped whimper might as well be a dinner bell. Both hog beasts grin and step forward, one swiping at Shade while the other stalks toward me. I'm about to scream at Shade again when the ground shakes, the very earth trembling.

I should be afraid as I fall onto my backside, but instead something inside me sighs in recognition. The earth shakes again, and this time the magic of it echoes through my bones. Without knowing how, I know who's causing this. *River.*

The hog beasts hesitate, their maws swiveling between the morsel that is me and whatever their preternatural senses are telling them is coming. And what's coming, I discover a heartbeat later, is three deadly fae males riding bareback at a full gallop.

Tye's hair streaks behind him, Coal's a tight bun atop his head. The latter dismounts with the horse still running, lands deftly on his feet, and steps between me and the hogs. River gallops around me, dirt from his horse's hooves spraying my face as he continues farther down the path, where more wet growls are now sounding. Tye, damn him, doesn't bother swerving and jumps his horse clear over my head before disappearing after River.

Coal's sword flashes, slicing the closest beast from crotch to neck in a single swipe before squaring off against the other.

Over my heart's pounding, I try to slither back from the

melee. With my life no longer in immediate peril, my body feels its injuries again and I whimper as my arm accidentally tries and fails to support my weight.

Shade jumps at the quiet sound and lopes toward me. The male's yellow eyes grip my gaze so tightly that I don't register anything odd until a heartbeat later, when I finally realize that while a wolf leapt into the air, it was a fae male who landed in a crouch beside me. Shining, shaggy black hair cascades down to his collarbone, where a gray sleeveless shirt hangs open to show a muscled chest narrowing into a taut abdomen.

A pair of familiar yellow eyes peers into my soul. "You are hurt," Shade says, his golden skin and broad shoulders filling the whole of my world.

8

LERALYNN

"Sh . . . Shade?" I manage.

The shock of seeing my wolf's fae features for the first time nearly crowds out the pain in my body. If possible, he is even more stunning than the other three, with high cheekbones, a full mouth, and a sharply carved jaw. The lines of his face are strong and smooth, as if chiseled out of marble, and his muscles ripple under his skin like silk in a breeze. So *this* is who shared my bed last night.

Shade runs his hands over my back and arm, his touch desperate. His nostrils flare, seeking out a scent. "You dislocated your shoulder," the male says, his face tight and both his hands still pressed against my skin as if he does not dare let go. His voice has a silky, songlike texture, studded with rough corners of disuse. "There is more, but we must leave Mystwood before seeing to it."

I whimper and pull back into myself as his hand slides to my forearm, jostling my hurt shoulder.

"I know, cub," Shade whispers into my ear, filling my nose with the scent of damp earth and rain. His shaggy, black hair is as thick as the wolf's was, his body a pulsing warmth that I remember from last night. His fingers brush my skin. "You need to let me set it. Hold my gaze and it will be over quickly."

I can't not hold Shade's gaze. His yellow eyes sparkle in the sunlight and fill an emptiness deep inside me, even as my entire body yells at me to flee. I try and fail to stay still as Shade's hands, warm and so large that I feel like a sprite beneath them, slide over my flesh.

He shifts my arm again, this time with firm intent.

I moan, struggling away from the hurt. "Don't. Please."

"I must, cub," Shade says, his breath caressing my cheek. "I know it hurts. Stay with me through the pain." His arms roll my limb firmly, ignoring my screams as my sinews stretch and shift and promise to tear and—something inside my shoulder pops into place and the pain recedes, leaving a dull, throbbing ache through my left side.

I wiggle my fingers and they respond obediently. My breath releases and Shade pulls me into his hard shoulder, stroking my hair in long, rhythmic strokes. Slow and warm and so very physical.

Once my breath calms, I gather myself together enough to pull away from the male. Only to regret it immediately as our surroundings rush back into focus—the ravaged carcasses of dead hog beasts, flies already buzzing over their spilled entrails, hoof tracks and uprooted grass, the other males now missing. Fighting. Because of me. "The others?" I manage to say.

A soft, confident chuckle. "They'll be fine."

I press my face back into Shade's shoulder, take three deep breaths, then pull away again—prepared this time. Shade releases me reluctantly, as if the loss of contact is hard for him to bear. I shift my leg until our knees touch and Shade seems to relax, crouching on the earth beside me.

"You shifted," I whisper.

Shade nods, his yellow eyes darkening. A deep pain flashes in his gaze and he turns his head away—though not before I can catch his face in my hands. After spending the night curled up with Shade's wolf, I feel at liberty to touch him more than I normally would. Shade holds still, allowing me to pull my palm along his cheek.

"Why now?" I ask, and he lifts his chin in challenge. "Why now, after ten years?"

"I couldn't exactly set your shoulder in wolf form, now could I?" says Shade.

"You could have not set my shoulder at all," I point out.

"No." He shakes his head forcefully. "Leaving you hurt was never an option, cub."

I swallow, the truth of his words penetrating through me. "Why?" I whisper. "I don't understand. I don't understand any of this."

Leaning close to me, Shade inhales a lungful of my scent and closes his eyes in a moment of contentment before brushing his lips softly over my cheek. "Because without you, we are only half-alive," he says into my ear. I blink, and by the time my eyes open again, Shade is rising to his feet, the squares of his abdomen shifting like building blocks beneath his skin. I'd have thought Shade's fae form would be hairy, but his chest is smooth, the only hint of hair confined to a few curly tufts peeking out from his low-riding trousers. Shade adjusts his waistband, which falls right back down to his hipbones.

My thighs tighten.

"I've lost some weight since I shifted," he mutters, and my face flames as I realize he followed the direction of my gaze perfectly. Abandoning the trousers to their fate, Shade stretches his arms behind his head and shakes like a wet dog dislodging drops of rain. His head cocks to one side and his eyes focus on something over my shoulder. "Coal is coming," he says.

I turn to see an empty forest, the three hog-beast carcasses the only sign of what happened. I shudder, remembering their growls, the hot breath on my neck in the endless moment before Shade arrived. I assumed Coal continued forward in the direction River and Tye had ridden, but apparently not. "You can smell him?" I ask.

Shade shakes his head. "My wolf could, but I can't in this form. The fae scent is stronger than a mortal's but nothing compared to my wolf's. I can hear Coal, though. He's stopped just beyond the bend to wait." A corner of his mouth lifts. "That's Coal being polite, giving me space." Squeezing my arm, Shade lifts his face. "Get over here, you bastard. And for stars' sake, keep downwind or even Lera will smell you."

Despite Shade's warning, I still gasp when Coal separates from the trees and steps onto the path a few paces away from us. He is covered with rust-colored blood and my eyes survey him from head to toe in search of injury. It takes me a moment to realize he's doing the same, and we look away when our eyes meet.

"Where are the others?" I ask in a thin voice, remembering that I'm the one who brought everyone into this mess.

"River and Tye are going to hunt down the sclice pack," Coal says, wiping his blade on his pants before storing it in a scabbard across his back. He wears a black sleeveless shirt, and his muscles shift with each smooth movement of his arms.

Apparently, none of the damn males are bothered by the cold. "It's worrisome that the beasts are coming this close to the mortal realm. Something to address with the Citadel when we get there, but for now a bit of cleanup."

I bite my lip. Coal speaks of the hog beasts as if they're a few unwanted rats. "Are . . . are there a great many of those things in Lunos?" I ask, trying to keep my voice steady.

Coal doesn't answer, our conversation apparently having stretched the limits of his tolerance for speaking with me. Turning to Shade, Coal gives the male a small nod. A *nod*. Some welcome back after a decade in wolf form. "Let's move her out of here."

Shade reaches for me, drawing me close quickly enough that, if I didn't know better, I'd think he were staking his claim. Within a moment, I find myself lifted off the ground and held against the male's chest, while Coal draws his blade and takes guard in the rear.

"I can walk," I protest. At least, I think I can.

Coal snorts.

"We aren't walking," Shade says into my hair, his arms tightening around my body as he starts into a lope that a mortal could never keep up with.

With the male's brutally efficient pace, we clear Mystwood quickly. Instead of setting course for the inn, however, Shade and Coal turn in the other direction, bringing us to a burbling creek about a mile south of our temporary residence. Wide, smooth stones form a basin of sorts, the water falling from above and filling the enclosure before leaving through a gap several paces wide. Shade settles me onto one of the broad stones but doesn't release me fully, one large hand remaining casually on the curve of my hip.

"Why are we here?" I ask.

"To bathe," says Shade, while Coal strips himself of bloody clothing, oblivious to both my presence and the cold. "We've caused enough of a commotion just lodging at the inn without showing up drenched in sclice blood. Plus, it's doubtful they have a tub big enough to fit any of us."

9

LERALYNN

My eyes widen as Coal pulls the shirt off his broad back, revealing corded muscles and taut skin. An intricate tattoo twines down the groove of his spine, and my fingers long to trace the pattern in hopes of learning its meaning. There are scars all over his back as well. Some long and thin, others jagged and wide, interrupting the ink. The legends say fae heal better than humans do. If that's true, the amount of force it took to leave those scars . . . My thoughts scramble away from Coal's back as the male removes his pants and tosses them on top of his boots and shirt.

The winged muscles of Coal's shoulder blades taper into a diamond-shaped lower back. The carved mounds of his buttocks complete the diamond's borders and round tightly before surrendering to honed hamstrings and calves. Coal might look like he's in his mid-twenties, but there are centuries of training, fighting, and killing lying beneath his skin.

Shade chuckles softly into my ear. "You'll find the fae less prudish than mortals," he says, while Coal slips into the water with a small splash.

I open my mouth to ask whether Tye and River will be able to find us, but the approach of two galloping riders, each leading a second horse, answers my question. Shade's arms tighten around me as the two approach, releasing me only when River pulls his mount to a rough halt and jumps off, his hand reaching toward me.

"Come here, Leralynn," River orders, the command in his voice sending a shiver through my core. River is taller and broader than the others—though considering that I don't clear the shoulders of any of them, River's additional size shouldn't make the difference it does. Maybe it isn't his size.

His jaw ticks and he steps toward me when I hesitate, his hands grasping my hips and lifting me into the air for a better look. "Are you all right?" he demands. "Talk to me, Leralynn."

My mouth is dry. I consider kicking him, but this would accomplish nothing—and hurt my foot. I brace my hands on his broad shoulders, which give off more heat than a woodstove. This close, River's dominating strength and shimmering wall of command give way to velvety skin, an intoxicating woodsy smell, and keen gray eyes that survey me with soul-clenching intensity.

"Am I in trouble?" I manage to say finally, my heart pounding. Maybe I should have added "sir" or "commander" to the end of that, but words are a scarce commodity just now. "For making everyone . . . come after me?"

River's brows narrow, studying my face. "Someone raised a hand to you in the past." Not a question. He shakes his head violently. "I don't strike humans, Leralynn. And even if I did, retribution is the farthest thing from my mind right now—I truly need to know that you are all right. There is no trick.

There is only you." His eyes widen as he stops speaking, a fleeting look crossing his face—almost like surprise at what just came out of his mouth.

I open my mouth but no words come. I wonder if River's magic includes turning me into a mute. If it does, Coal must be jealous.

A second pair of hands pulls me from River's grip, and the scent of pine and citrus washes over me as my back hits a hard chest. "If you are looking for someone to ride, Lilac Girl," Tye whispers, "at least I can promise not to dump you off in a nest of sclices."

I elbow the male behind me, cursing as I hit the sting point and my arm goes numb.

Tye chuckles and sets me back on the ground, his arms still pressing me against him. "Come," he says. "I smell blood on you, lass. And some of it is yours."

I'm about to protest, but a glance up shows River and Shade facing each other with arms crossed, their gazes exchanging more than words. Tye might enjoy being obnoxious, but he knows when to give his friends space—as well as when to rescue me from his commander's attention. Settling me on one of the larger boulders, Tye crouches down to unbuckle my boots, his green eyes level with mine.

"What were those hog-beast things?" I ask, shivering at the memory of salivating fangs and the stench of rotten meat.

"Sclices." Tye pulls my right boot off and runs his hands expertly over my shin and ankle. Under his wide, rough palms, I look pale, delicate. The latter of which I can't afford to be as part of this quint. Satisfied that both are in one piece, he moves on to the second. "Mors's version of rodents. They infested Mystwood a few centuries back and it's been a chore to keep them contained. Dress off, bonny lass. We are going for a swim."

I hug my arms around my shoulders. "You can go wherever the hell you like. I am waiting for a bathtub."

"Not an option," says River, now crouching beside Tye. "Sclices are attracted to their own blood. Returning to the inn as we are would be like ringing a dinner bell. The rodents should be unable to leave Mystwood, but no wards are foolproof." River grins, showing a set of sharp canines that utterly reverse any calming effect his tone might otherwise have had. "Plus, Shade smells wounds on you. He won't let you out of his sight until he makes certain you are whole. That's the hazard of having a wolf along." The grin fades slowly, and River's gray gaze lowers to the ground for a heartbeat before swinging up slowly to pierce my soul. When he speaks next, his voice is low and raw. "Thank you for calling Shade back to us. I owe you a debt. We all do."

I didn't do anything. I swallow. "Do all of you shift into animals?" I ask, veering away from a conversation I don't begin to understand. I examine River with narrowed eyes. "You would be a lion. Coal, I imagine, would be . . ." I turn to Tye. "Which animal kills first and considers why it bothered later? It must be something from your world."

Tye throws back his head and laughs, the sun playing in his eyes.

I'm so mesmerized by the rich sound that I fail to notice River leaning forward to scoop me up until my body is already in the air, my legs kicking. "Bath time," the bastard intones just as he tosses me right into the freezing pool.

The icy cold steals my breath the moment I hit the water, paralyzing my vocal cords for several heartbeats. My limbs flail, my back arching against the chill. Once I can draw a lungful of air, however, I screech loudly enough to—if the fates are with me—shatter the immortals' delicate hearing.

The water beside me explodes in a fountain of freezing spray. I jump back, my toes vaguely discovering the pool's bottom as a still-clothed, furiously shaking Tye rises from the liquid depths. He is tall enough that the water only reaches his waist, whereas it laps at my collarbone. Tye's red hair is plastered to his face and his green eyes flash murder at River, who is still ashore and disrobing calmly.

"It seemed only fair," River calls, placidly unrepentant.

Tye growls.

I turn my back on River just as the quint commander starts undoing his fly, and I find myself looking at Shade's naked chest. His black hair spills over his shoulders, dripping water onto a muscled chest, where his nipples are as erect from the cold as mine. The pectorals themselves are harsh, slightly rounded rectangles, contoured perfectly to fit into a girl's palm.

"Cold?" Shade asks. He holds his arms out to me and I walk to him like a mouse into a snake's maw, too hypnotized to think. Shade's hands encircle my ribcage and lift me up in a smooth motion, settling me comfortably on his hips. My legs wrap around his waist for balance, one of my heels settling into the groove atop his right buttock. The heat of his body seeps through my wet shirt, and I give up all pretense of propriety in favor of pressing myself against him.

"Tye," Shade calls over my shoulder, and I feel a second large body approach me from the back. Hands reach for me and there is a sharp ripping sound that I realize too late is my dress. Shade's warm hand finds the back of my neck, his other arm still supporting my hips. I've never been so mindful of my body as I am now, every soft curve and inch of smooth skin making itself known for the first time and singing in awareness. "Easy, cub. Sclices aren't known for their hygiene, and one of them marked you deeper than any of us like."

Tye's calloused fingers caress my bare back, pouring water from a cupped hand over my tender skin. I have one more brief notion of a struggle, but the cold, the fatigue, and the males' bullheaded resolve finally win over. I bury my face in Shade's neck, savoring the way his earth-and-rain scent mixes with Tye's pine and citrus, while the immortals wash away the morning's nightmare.

COAL

*C*oal turned his back on Lera. It was all he could do not to run his hands all over her body, checking every bone, every fragile mortal joint. When she'd brought the stallion out from his stall that morning, Coal had been curious, watching from his room's window as the girl went about brushing down the animal. He'd still been curious when he saw the boy bring the saddle, and when she'd mounted, settling that tight backside into the saddle in a way he knew excruciatingly well, her fiery hair whipping around her face in the breeze.

He'd watched it all with a male's irrepressible curiosity. And then it was too late.

Coal's fingers curled into fists. He should have known better. He did know better. Czar, the stallion, was sensitive as all hell, with speed and muscle to match his opinionated spirit. Coal had fully expected Czar to dump Lera on the sand—he'd not counted on her hanging on when he bolted. The mortal had more tenacity and courage than any of the quint, himself included, had given her credit for.

"Are you all right?" River asked, slipping into the pool beside Coal. The waterfall's cascade drummed a steady rhythm, but the quint commander spoke quietly nonetheless. Coal wasn't surprised at the question, which didn't mean he welcomed it either. But that was River for you. The commander knew when something was off—he made it his bloody business to know. River's eyes were soft now and saw more of Coal than he wanted them to.

Coal glanced over his shoulder, assuring himself that the girl was still in one piece. She was. And with the way Lera's wet clothes clung to her body, Coal was immediately grateful for the freezing water. Her breasts, while not especially large, were firm and perfectly matched to the sinful bend of her hips —which Shade was presently supporting. Her eyes, a liquid chocolate, glowed against her pale face and wet hair, making her look like the predator she didn't know she was.

Turning his back to the mortal once more, Coal grabbed his clothes and scrubbed them, watching the water around the cloth turn rusty brown before flowing clear again. "I'm fine," he said curtly. "Save your 'it's not real' reminders for Shade and Tye. I'm fully aware."

River rubbed his face, a flicker of pain flashing in his gray eyes. The commander let Coal see more than he showed the others, and Coal respected the male enough to never comment on it unless River himself asked. "I fear I'm the one who needs reminding," said River. "When I realized she was in Mystwood, what could happen to her, a piece of my soul howled in fear. And when we entered the forest . . ."

"I felt it too," Coal said, his attention on the laundry. "The new power coursing through me once we were free of the mortal realm." *More power than I felt when Kai was alive,* Coal didn't add. "Mistake or not, for now she completes the quint."

River ran a hand through his hair. A tell. Coal's commander was wrestling with something and needed time to find the words.

"When I came up to her," River said finally, "she feared that I intended to punish her for starting this, for putting the others in danger."

"A fair inquiry." Coal wrung out his hair and knotted it back into a bun. "If it were Tye, you would have had his hide. What did you say?"

"The truth," River ground out. "I couldn't even bring myself to imply otherwise." The male's fists tightened. "I had an opportunity to say something ominous, to remind her how dangerous we are. Keep her from getting attached."

"You mean to remind her how dangerous *you* are." Coal crossed his arms. "Don't sell me your horseshit, River. You've found some noble reason to frighten away every female since Daz left. You're just annoyed that, this time, you failed."

River blew out a slow breath. "She deserves better than this, Coal. We bring her pain and danger, and she brings us Shade and strength."

Coal pulled himself out of the basin and pulled on his wet breeches, letting the cold air sting his skin. It was his horse who'd taken off with the girl this morning, and Coal doubted it was coincidence that of all the horses to try and conquer, the girl had chosen that one. River was right, and Coal wanted to give Lera something. Except that the one thing Coal could offer wasn't nearly as pleasant as Shade's comfort or Tye's smiles. "I want to train her."

"To do what?" River asked.

Coal pulled on his shirt. "To ride, to defend herself, to be a force in her own right. To do all those things that no one teaches you when you're a slave." He hadn't meant to say the latter part aloud, but River was discreet enough to feign deafness. The quint commander was royal born, trained to defend and protect since before the magic ever summoned him to the Citadel. He didn't know what being truly helpless felt like. Coal did. "We owe her that."

River frowned, his gaze examining Lera before returning to Coal. "I don't imagine she will thank you for the experience. Not at first."

Coal's jaw tightened. No, the mortal would little enjoy it. But she had Shade and Tye to soothe away the aches; she didn't need Coal to do the same thing. Not that he would even know how.

River sighed. "We could all—"

Coal snorted, directing River's gaze to where their quint brothers cared for Lera's wound. "Tye and Shade won't have the heart to push her, and you have other responsibilities." Coal started for his horse. Someone had to ride to the inn to fetch fresh clothes, and he needed the time to think anyway. "We all have our strengths," he called to River over his shoulder. "Being liked isn't mine."

As Coal mounted his horse, a part of him wondered whether his whole idea wasn't actually rooted in preventing Lera from sharing his saddle again, which last time had left Coal's cock throbbing painfully the whole night.

11

LERALYNN

*T*here is a set of beautifully made leather-reinforced riding breeches waiting for me outside the door when I wake up the following morning, together with a soft tunic, a pair of fine hard-heeled boots, and an ill-humored Coal. Wearing his usual black in contrast to his blond hair, Coal leans against the wall, his legs crossed one over the other as he studies me with slightly hooded eyes. He looks fresh and alert—and breathtakingly gorgeous. Damn him.

"Who do I have to thank for the clothes?" I ask, running my hands down the supple brown leather. One of the males must have taken my measurements and spent a small fortune to acquire the pieces on short notice. I've never owned anything this fine before, and a small part of me is appalled at the thought of getting the fabric dirty.

Coal shrugs one rock-hard shoulder in a "don't know, don't care" gesture. "River wants to sweep the area for more sclices, so we are staying put for the day. I wanted to see whether we'd need a cart for when we do move out."

"A cart?" I raise a brow. "For what?"

"For you." Coal picks at his nails. "You ride like a sack of grain, so we might as well transport you like one."

"Are you being an ass on purpose," I croon, "or are you always this delightful in the morning?"

Coal growls softly, showing his canines. Of the four males, I think Coal is the most immediately deadly, the one willing to inflict—and take—more damage than the others. "Do you want me to teach you to ride or not?"

My eyes widen even as my chest tightens in excitement. After yesterday's disaster, I imagined the males wouldn't let me near a horse, much less offer to help. I cross my arms. The offer, like the clothes, smells too good to be true. "Shouldn't you be off chasing sclices?" I ask, stepping behind my door to pull on the pants and boots. "Killing slobbery monsters seems more in line with your preferences than teaching a mortal how not to topple from a horse."

"We pulled straws and I lost," says Coal.

I step back into the hall. "Liar."

Coal holds up four fingers, bending them back one at a time as he speaks. "Shade spooks any horse he goes near, River's in charge and gets first dibs on the good stuff, and Tye . . . Tye is Tye."

"What does that mean?" I raise a brow.

Coal snorts. "It means that it will snow in midsummer before any of us leave Tye alone with a female and expect anything vertical to take place."

My face heats and I brush past Coal toward the staircase, jogging lightly down its rickety steps. The scent of coffee and fresh bread tempts me as I rush past the kitchen, but with Coal as finicky as a bloody bride, I'm not about to jeopardize my chance at learning to ride for the sake of breakfast. It's been a while since anyone taught me anything, Zake's belt-driven lessons on punctuality and work ethic notwithstanding. Mimi teaching me to read when I was younger comes to mind, though it did me little good for lack of books. I swallow, common sense dampening foolish enthusiasm. I'll take what Coal offers, but I'll expect there to be a price. There always is.

The stable boy is already holding a saddled horse when we walk out to the barn. Not Czar, I note with disappointment, but a dapple gelding whose brown eyes evaluate me suspiciously. Beyond the stalls, a freshly cleaned paddock stands with an open gate. Taking the gelding's reins, I thank the boy and watch him race away from Coal as quickly as if he'd just filched a roll. With our audience thus gone, I lift my arm to pat the horse's neck and feel a jolt of pain from the fall. Shade set the shoulder, but the muscles are tight and sore. My stomach shifts, the memory of the wild gallop, the hard ground, the jolting pain suddenly all too vivid.

"I can smell your fear, you know," Coal says lazily behind me. "The horse can too."

"Do you want me to bathe?" I ask over my shoulder.

Coal chuckles, the resulting dimple on his cheek transforming his face from handsome to downright unfair. His eyes are more sky blue than stormy ocean today, and I wonder whether it means something. It must, because a bit of my fear melts away. *Today is different*, my mind whispers. *Today, you are not alone.*

Taking the horse from me, Coal holds the gelding under the chin. "Mount up," he orders.

Right. With the mounting block I used yesterday nowhere in sight, I raise my right foot, only to discover the stirrup much higher than I imagined and hop about until I finally manage to stick my toe into the little wooden box. At which point a new problem emerges: The only way I can mount now would have me facing the horse's rump.

Coal raises a brow at me.

"You could have told me I was starting with the wrong foot before I got here," I tell him, removing my right foot from its hard-won hold and replacing it with my left. This time, when my toes find the stirrup, the bloody horse takes one step to the side, rendering all my efforts in vain. I finally manage to haul myself into the saddle, only to nearly fall over the other side when the horse shifts his weight. My breath catches. "I'm all right," I tell Coal once I can breathe again. "In case that matters."

"It really doesn't," says Coal. Liar. I can see him already reconsidering the wisdom of allowing me on horseback. Clipping the end of a long, coiled rope to the horse's headstall, Coal clicks his tongue and the animal obediently starts moving in a circle around him.

I grip onto the mane. "Wait. Don't you want to tell me how to control him first? Where are the reins?"

"You don't get reins," Coal calls out to me. He clicks his tongue and the horse turns into an earthquake. "I control the horse. You stay on."

I don't stay on.

I fall. Over and over and over again, until my eyes water and sand from the paddock works itself into every crevice of my clothing. It isn't fun or exciting or anything I expected it to be.

Told you as much, a dark part of my mind cackles, even as Coal issues more orders.

"Heels down, head up, mortal. Not the other bloody way around."

I climb back into the saddle, my body shaking.

Coal's voice is hard, merciless. As if falling, not riding, was the day's expectation all along. "You do know the difference between up and down?"

"You are an ass," I tell him, gripping the saddle as he starts the horse trotting again.

"So the grain sack speaks." Coal clicks his tongue and the horse quickens. "Let go of the saddle, grain sack. Holding the pommel shifts your balance. Head up. Get your heels off his sides unless—"

The horse's muscles bunch and he leaps into a sprint. I scream and fall to the sand, rolling away from the thundering hooves. Stars damn it. Two bloody hours. I've been falling for two hours, my body is one large bruise, and my stomach growls in starvation. The damn males made riding look easy, the horses living extensions of their powerful bodies. I strike the ground with my palm, sending clumps of sand into the air.

"Are you here to train or throw a tantrum?" Coal glares at me from above.

"Screw you," I hiss back.

"Get up, grain sack."

I swipe the back of my hand over my mouth.

"Get. Up." The pitch of Coal's voice is low, the demand harsh as ice. Eyes still on me, he retrieves the gelding and whistles for the stable boy, handing off the horse while I'm still finding my feet. "You've lost your riding privileges until you can prove to me that you are not a whiny child incapable of controlling her emotions."

I dust my clothes off and glare silently at Coal. If he thinks he is going to scare me into surrendering, into becoming their tame little piece of human chattel to drag to the Citadel for castration, he can bloody think again. Yes. My hands curl into fists, the inferno of fury burning self-pity to a crisp. "I await your instruction, O Great One."

"Since you appear so fond of falling, we will work on that," Coal says coolly. "Chin down when you hit the sand, and slap it with your arm. Another of your favorite tricks, I've noted. You'll be a natural."

I give him a vulgar gesture.

Coal seizes my arm and launches me through the air. I have one moment to realize that I'm flying before the ground rises up to meet me and I land hard on my back, the impact echoing through every abused bone and muscle. My breath hitches, making me fight for air.

"Chin down. Slap the sand," Coal repeats, as if my problem lies with my hearing. "Get up and do it again."

I don't want to. It was bad enough falling from horseback when the goal was to stay on. Now there is no chance of not slamming into the ground. I climb up to my knees, the world swaying a bit, and swallow, my eyes finally stinging. Maybe that's what Coal was aiming for all along.

I am not going to cry, I shout in my mind, my teeth sinking into my lip hard enough to draw blood.

Coal lowers to one knee beside me. "What did you imagine would happen, mortal?" he demands softly. "Did you imagine you were joining an embroidery guild? That there would be no pain? No bruises? No feeling like you'd rather die than work a moment longer but doing it anyway?"

"I thought I'd have a chance," I whisper.

"You don't." Coal rises, dusting off his pants. "Come find me when you are ready to work."

12

LERALYNN

I wait for Coal to leave before trudging back to the inn. My hair is damp with sweat, and now that I am not moving, the wind threatens to freeze the strands right off my head. I scurry toward my room, spending the last of my remaining life energy hauling myself up the steps, not realizing that someone is in my way until my forehead smacks right into a muscled chest.

"You can still walk?" Tye says with a click of his tongue. "Coal must be going a wee soft."

I glare at the male.

Tye's face splits into an unabashed grin. "You look adorable with murder in your eyes, Lilac Girl."

"I thought you were out sclice hunting," I mutter. "I was hoping they'd maul you."

"No you weren't." Tye scoops me up with an arm behind my knees and shoulder blades and carries me the rest of the way to my room, where he sets me on the bed. "You like me too much to want me mauled by sclices."

"A situation that is changing rapidly," I mutter.

Tye grabs one of my legs and pulls it across his lap, deftly untying my bootlaces to free my foot from the shoe. His hand brushes casually over my ankle in a motion I'd think nothing about if he'd not done the same thing yesterday. He's checking me for injuries. My brows pull together, my muddled thoughts slowly coalescing. "Are you really here by happenstance, or were you waiting for me to crawl away from Coal's morning workout?"

Tye blinks too innocently to be believable, and I cross my arms, glaring at the redheaded male.

He leans back on outstretched hands. "And if I were? Would it be so terrible if we wanted to check that one of our own is still in one piece?"

One of our own. The words pierce my soul, permeating through me like liquor on a cold day. I shake off the allure. "If you care about the number of pieces I'm in, would it not have been wiser to keep Coal from trying to kill me to begin with?" I ask reasonably.

Tye laughs. "If Coal were trying to kill you, lass, you'd be very, very dead now. As it is, the field between feeling like you might prefer to be dead and actually being dead is much vaster than you imagine. And Coal has explored every dark inch of it." Tye adds the last part quietly, as if unsure he wants to say it at all.

I frown, but before I can press Tye on it, the male is leaning forward again, looming over me. Unlike River, who seems to use his size on purpose to keep order in the world around him, Tye has the air of a good-natured mastiff who can't be held responsible for his considerable bulk. Reaching over, he straightens the high neckline of my tunic, the origins of which are still a mystery.

"What are you doing now?" I ask suspiciously.

Tye winces. "Trying to conjure a way of tricking you into taking off your shirt," he confesses, holding up his hands as I strike him with a pillow. "I promised Shade to check on your shoulder and the other cuts."

I cross my arms. "And is there anything else on your agenda? Spill it, Tye."

He shifts his weight. "Just remember that I am one of four males," he says cautiously. "You can't blame me for everyone's requests."

"How much do you want to bet on that?" I ask, glaring into his green eyes—though staying angry at Tye takes a great deal of effort. No wonder the four bastards chose him. "Spill it. Now."

"Shade is worried about your shoulder. And River is concerned that we know too little about mortals' fragility, how slowly you heal. And Coal—"

"Coal is in on this too?" I fall back onto my bed. "Coal was the one tormenting me all morning. If he was so worried, he could have backed the bloody hell off."

"If it's of any consolation, Coal little cares about what damage he left on you this morning. His concern was about the damage your former master might have inflicted."

Zake. It doesn't make me feel better. I give Tye a dark look.

Tye shuts his eyes. "This is not going how I'd planned," he confesses. He blows out a long breath, and when he looks at me next, there is a twinkle of mischief in that green gaze. He surveys me quickly from head to toe, then holds out his hand. "Let's put the plan to get you undressed on hold and do something else instead," he offers.

"What?" I accept his hand in spite of myself and he pulls me up easily. I should kick him in the shins for his original intentions regarding my clothes, but there is so much life and good nature in Tye's eyes that I can't help the curiosity.

Tye's grin widens. "I think we should go see what Coal and the others are doing," he says, tossing my boots back into my arms.

With curiosity winning over soreness, I pull my boots back on and gratefully accept Tye's warm cloak, which he claims to have little need of. With a gentle guiding hand along the small of my back, Tye ushers me downstairs, through the kitchen, where I catch him pilfering a sweet roll and cheese, and back outside.

Tye hands me the food, which I devour quickly, the bliss of warm bread in my belly momentarily distracting me from where we are headed—which is right back to the paddock I was recently dismissed from.

Instead of being empty, the paddock appears to be hosting three large males armed with wooden blades. Despite the cold, the males are all shirtless, sweat slithering lazily down the grooves of their muscled backs. Coal dances at the center of the lot, his practice blade and body a blur as he battles at once against River and Shade. River is the tallest, but Coal is the fiercest, blue eyes blazing with singular focus. Red marks from missed parries cover all the males' flesh, and I flinch as Shade darts in, low and lithe like the wolf he's been for ten years, and paints another stripe across Coal's shoulders while the male is busy blocking a skull-splitting attack from River.

Not even flinching from the blow, Coal twists around to thrust his sword tip into Shade's taut abdomen. Shade stumbles back, his arm pressed against his middle as he falls to one knee, watching River and Coal circle each other while his own shoulders heave with exhaustion and pain.

Tye's hand clamps over my mouth before I can shout

Shade's name. "He's all right," Tye promises, his arms encircling my body, keeping me from rushing into the ring. "A bit out of practice fighting in his fae form is all. Watch."

True to Tye's prediction, Shade climbs back to his feet after a few moments, adjusts his sword grip, and circles the melee in search of an opening. Noting Shade's return, Coal gives his quint brother a curt nod before attempting to murder him all over again.

I turn, burying my face in Tye's shoulder, and feel a rumbling chuckle vibrate his chest. "Stupid masochistic immortal *males*."

"We worry about you just as fiercely, Lilac Girl," Tye answers, pulling me back enough to peer into my face. "More. We know what damage to a fae body looks like, what our flesh can handle. You are something else entirely. Fragile but resilient and . . . stars, it's enough to make us go mad, smelling pain on you and not knowing how to relieve it, how bad the damage might be."

His grin fades but his gaze remains on me, drinking in every line of my face as I drink in his. Tye's hair is fiery in the sun and his deep green eyes reflect the rays, which bounce against his shiny black lashes.

My heart pauses then leaps from my chest, beating so hard against my ribs that I feel the vibrations all the way through my core. Tye's pine-and-citrus scent spreads through me with each breath, lighting each of my nerves. I'm suddenly aware of every bit of his presence, the steady pressure of his powerful arm on the small of my back, the rise and fall of his broad chest, the flop of red hair that sways just over his left eye.

Tye's breath caresses the top of my head, ruffling my hair.

Behind me, the steady *clank clank clank* of practice blades continues to echo from the paddock, punctuated by the occasional grunt of too much maleness clashing. Not violence, I think—though it would be foolish to think of these males as anything but deadly predators—but synergy.

I raise my hand to Tye's cheek, shaved smooth and sculpted into an angled jaw. His cheekbones are chiseled to perfect symmetry, except for a touch of freckles on the right, so faint that you have to be this close to see them. A hidden mark of mischief that is thoroughly Tye.

Tye shuts his eyes. "Stars, Lera," he says through clenched teeth. "Have you no notion of what you're doing to me?"

My fingertip bounces between his freckles before shifting to trace his jaw.

The male beneath my hands goes statue still.

"Do you mind it?" I ask.

Tye barks a strangled laugh, his hands suddenly tightening around me. "I mind that I can't take you right here," he rasps into my ear, out bodies fitting together like pieces of a long-lost puzzle. After a heartbeat, Tye's hand slides up to grip the back of my neck, the other palming my hip and pulling me even closer.

I raise my face to his, rising up on my toes as my lips part.

Tye hisses. The mirth in his eyes disappears, a primal need burning in its place. "Step away from me, lass," he rasps, his voice half warning, half plea. "I can't keep myself in check much longer."

I tighten my hands around Tye's arms instead, my fingers digging mercilessly into his hard biceps. The need in Tye's gaze seeps through his skin into mine, lighting a flame inside my core. I can't think. Can't move. I *want*.

A growl escapes Tye's chest and his mouth descends with a predator's claim. Warm lips lock onto mine, forcing my mouth to yield to his demand, to my own visceral need. The tip of

Tye's tongue skims the top of my teeth, sending a shiver down my body.

I moan against Tye's mouth and his fingers tighten on the nape of my neck, nails gripping my flesh as mine mark his. I press against him, my heart galloping.

His mouth moves again and—

Cold air hits me suddenly as Tye's body is ripped away. I blink, the world coming reluctantly into focus to reveal Tye now flat on his back with River's boot in the middle of his chest and the tip of River's practice blade pointed at Tye's jugular.

LERALYNN

"Get off him." I shove River's chest with all my might, which has absolutely no effect on the male except for a curious twitch of his eyes as I stumble backward into Shade, who keeps me from falling on my ass. Regaining my footing, I step right back up to River and glare into his gray eyes, meeting that thunderous storm inside him head-on.

Oh, he *is* furious. Furious enough to let the anger slip through the cold of command.

Back at the stream, he promised not to lay a hand on me, but plainly that didn't apply to the other quint-bonded under his command. To his real warriors.

That quickly, that stupidly, I don't want River's promise. Just as Shade's touch soothed a jagged loneliness inside of me, the intensity of River's icy, dominating energy also finds a mate inside my soul. A fire inside me that I didn't know existed.

Ice and flame. Our wills meet in a clash of power and fury

that is as terrifying as it is irresistible. "I said," my voice sounds too vivid to be mine, "get. Off."

River's dark eyes flash. He isn't used to being challenged, it appears. And likely with good reason. A small growl escapes his chest.

An answering growl sounds behind me, but I shake my head at Shade without ever breaking River's gaze. The newly born essence inside me doesn't want Shade's protection—it wants to dance with River. Welcomes it. Longs for it. Because that part of me senses that beneath River's impenetrable wall of muscle and order is a spirit worth tangling with.

River's chest expands with deep, still-panting breaths. He is shirtless from the sparring match, a thin sheen of sweat covering his sun-kissed skin and glistening enticingly. His short dark hair spikes off his head with moisture, and as he cools off, his nipples grow as taut as the carved squares of his abdomen. He steps toward me, each movement filled with a lethal immortal grace that should frighten me but does not.

"You don't understand fae," River tells me, centuries of knowledge and training backing each of his words. The commander's sheer size is overwhelming. Made more so by his ethereal beauty and the fact that my face barely reaches his sternum. "You've no notion of what this can do to us. But this village idiot does." This time, River bares his teeth at Tye, who has quietly picked himself up and now watches from the sidelines.

"Then maybe you should growl a bit less and talk a bit more," I tell River, raising my chin while the other males exchange glances ranging from amused to worried. I step closer to River, though it means tilting my head back to keep our gazes locked. "If you want me to understand, then *explain*."

River's brows flicker, and to my utter shock, he tilts his head to the side, considering my words. "That . . . that is a fair request," he says with a curt nod. Turning to Coal, River holds out his hand for a second practice sword, which Coal obediently tosses to him. "Will you join me in the paddock, Leralynn?"

My eyes narrow and I'm about to explain the difference between talking and beating me to a pulp when River shakes his head.

"I'm not going to spar with you," he says, dismissing the others with a short jerk of his chin. "I simply wish to occupy my hands with something while we speak, and it is polite to offer you a blade as well if I have one."

Accepting Coal's blade, I follow River into the empty ring and watch quietly as he swings at a rope-wrapped post that I'd originally dismissed as something to hang feed buckets on. One strike. Two. Five. Each a dull, clean thud that the post swallows without protest. "Do you imagine we are like humans?" River says finally. "Just with pointy ears, longer lifespans, and a bit of magic in our veins?"

"I don't know what you are," I confess. I don't know what I am either. Not anymore. I twirl my sword—River was right, it *is* nice to have something in my hands while we talk.

"We are predators," River says with no hint of apology. "Our instincts heightened—our senses, our drive to hunt, to protect, to mate. A bonfire of need and desire, compared to a human's mere candle."

I nod my understanding. The bond with the males has woken something primal in me as well, though I've not worked out what or how.

River attacks his target, his movements fluid. "We control it, the aggression and emotion, but it's a constant, simmering battle against the animals that our instincts scream at us to be. If you were . . . to become Tye's female, the territorial predator in him would not abide the threat to his claim that the rest of the males in the quint pose." River strikes the training post again, and the wooden target wavers in the earth from the impact. Again. Again. River's grip on his practice sword is hard enough to bleach his knuckles. "Shade, Coal, me," River punctuates each name with a blow, knocking the post further from its deep hole, "none of us would dare come near you for fear of the consequences. Until we damn the consequences to hell and it tears us all apart into shattered bits." River spins, his blade an extension of his powerful body as he rips the training post free of the ground.

He stands heaving, his eyes on the downed target as his chest and shoulders rise and fall with each gasp of cool air. "I don't expect you to understand," he says finally. "Your very presence, it—"

I'm moving before I can think, my hand reaching up to clutch River's sweat-slicked shoulder, twisting the male around to face me. My eyes meet River's gray ones, and for one split second he allows me to see the caustic fear in them. *Me*, I realize. This powerful immortal is afraid of me, of what I could do to his quint—to his world.

My heart tears. Placing my free hand against River's face, I press my palm tightly against his cheek. "I am not Tye's female," I say firmly. "I belong to me. And I am the quint's too, just as the quint is mine. Until this Citadel of yours severs our tether, we are an *us*—no matter who kisses whom."

River's whole body stills, the tension singing in his coiled muscles. "You . . . you can't possibly mean that," he says, trying and failing to check the budding hope in his voice.

Rising onto my toes, I brush my lips against his cheek. "I claim you as mine, River," I tell him softly. "You and Tye and Coal and Shade. Whatever comes, we will face it together."

LERALYNN

*R*iver, Tye, and Shade return to sclice hunting in the afternoon, Coal again seeming to have drawn the short straw of being left behind with me. Because who wouldn't want to fight slobbering hog things as post-lunch entertainment? We both watch in silence as the others ride off, then turn to weigh each other. Around us, the inn grounds and common room are quiet, guests who were here when we arrived having either chosen or been paid to relocate.

Still shirtless from his earlier practice and apparently impervious to the cold, Coal is leaning against the stable's outer wall, his broad shoulders threatening to bow the old wood. Well-worn black breeches hang on his hip crests, the V of his abdomen disappearing into the dangerously low waistline. His long blond hair is tied back into a tight bun that my unwieldy locks would never abide. He crosses his arms over his chest and my gaze narrows at something I'd not noticed before.

After three hundred years of fighting, the scars on Coal's

lithe body are understandable, but the ones circling his wrists are something else entirely. Someone shackled him. Held him for so long, rubbing the binds so deep, that Coal's immortal body never fully repaired the cuts. My mouth dries, my hand aching to brush over his wrist, as if touch could erase the hurt.

I hadn't realized just how deeply I meant my words when I told River that I claim all the quint brothers as my own.

Coal's gaze follows mine and hardens, a sudden chill settling over him. The male raises his chin, his eyes flashing with a challenge. I might have told River that I'm claiming the four males as mine, but that doesn't mean they all wish to claim me in return.

Not that I'm giving up on Coal without a fight. "Are we training or talking?" I ask.

He cocks a brow. "Careful what you ask for, mortal. Tye and Shade aren't here to coddle you now."

I take a step toward him, close enough that the sudden scent of male musk washes over me, Coal's sculpted pectorals and shoulders making me feel absurdly small. "Scared to work without their spotting?" I ask, my voice huskier than usual.

He swallows, the apple of his throat bobbing, even as his hands tighten into fists that I'm certain I'm not intended to notice. "Get on the sand."

My pulse quickens as I walk the twenty paces to the paddock we trained in earlier, my body still aching from the falls. I must have hit my head harder than I thought during one of those tumbles, because there is no reason any sane being would goad Coal into a repeat performance otherwise.

Coal clears the paddock fence with a smooth jump, not even breaking stride, while I use the gate like normal people do. People. Coal isn't people. None of the quint are.

"So, what—"

The rest of my question dissolves into a choked *oomph* as Coal launches himself at me, his shoulder knocking me cleanly back onto the sand. The fall is hard enough to take my breath, and I swallow a whimper as I stare up at the male, whose chest is heaving slightly faster than it should.

So we are playing throw-Lera-around again. At least I know this game. I wait for Coal to get off me, even as an idiotic part of me hates the thought of losing physical contact. As brutal as Coal is, I feel safer with him than I ever did with Zake.

Except for the part where he is still on top of me. "Get off," I growl.

"Make me."

I buck beneath him. Once. Twice. The futility of it sinks through me with each failing twitch of muscle. "Get off," I say again. Coal's weight, always considerable, is feeling heavier than it did moments ago, the heat from his body shoving itself into me. The world seems to shrink around us and it's a struggle to draw breath, to assure myself that there is breath to draw. "Get the hell off! I'm not jesting, Coal."

He shifts, becoming heavier and hotter still. His face moves in line with mine, our noses touching. "Neither am I," Coal says, showing sharp canines. "Make me."

My heart stutters, a sharp lash of panic bursting through my veins. I can't. I can't move him. I can't breathe. I can't . . . My teeth grind together, my weakness pressing on my chest as much as Coal's weight. I was wrong. Coal isn't safe at all. Stars. He wants me gone, away from his quint brothers, away from his life. He wants to be hunting right now, not minding a useless girl.

"Do something, mortal," Coal growls. "Save your hide."

I shut my eyes, bracing myself for the inevitable pain.

Despite the sand beneath me, I'm back at Zake's stable, cowering against a stall while he bruises me for imagined misdeeds. For not wanting him. *Zake wants me to submit. Even Mimi says I should. Everyone says I should.* I shudder, my heart pounding so quickly that the hard-won gasps of air aren't enough.

The weight atop me disappears, and as quickly as I was on the ground, I'm now in the air, Coal's powerful hands gripping my shoulders. The male's blue eyes flash with a fury I've never seen as he lifts me to his eye level, my feet dangling off the ground.

"You never do that again," Coal shouts, his nostrils flaring. "You never stop fighting. You understand?"

I swallow, my mind sluggishly trudging from the darkness.

Coal shakes me, but there is a difference in the motion from how it should feel. A desperation and fear that I mistook for anger. "I can teach you to fight," Coal tells me. "I can teach you to defend yourself. I can teach you a thousand things you can do. I can't make you want to do any of them." He releases me quickly, like a hot coal, setting me back on my feet before crouching on the sand himself, his head braced in his hands.

The marks on Coal's wrists fill my vision. Thick white scars encircling the tender skin.

I wrap my arms around myself, cold now. "I thought you wanted me to surrender to you," I whisper—whether in apology or explanation, I don't know.

His face jerks up, fast like the predator he is. "I never want you to surrender to me, Lera. Not to me, not to anyone. You are too good for that." Coal rises to his feet, smooth like a panther, and steps back toward me until his musky, metallic scent caresses my cheeks. His chest expands and lowers with deep, powerful breaths, even as his arms rise tentatively to my shoulders. For a male who just used his weight to make me whimper in misery, the care with which he touches my skin is shudderingly intense.

Coal's touch sends a thousand sparks through me, but it's his eyes that capture me now. I thought they were just blue, but they are more complex than that, with specks of amethyst around the irises that turn brilliant when the light hits them right.

"What now?" I whisper, my voice hitching because I know the answer. Now is when Coal turns and washes his hands of the mortal girl who is too weak for him.

His breath stills, his hand trailing up to take my chin. "Are you afraid of me, Lera?" he asks.

I open my mouth and shut it without answering, the storm inside too loud to discern. I'm not scared of Coal. But I should be. What do I do with that? I bite my lip. "Do you want me to be?"

He lets out a long breath, closing his eyes for a heartbeat. "I should." He growls softly—though the warning seems to be for himself, not me—and catches my eyes again. "But I prefer trust. If you could trust me to train you, to make you very, very uncomfortable in the ring . . . I'd prefer you be a bit afraid of that, but not of me."

LERALYNN

There is a wolf on my bed when I trudge up to my room in the evening, my whole body one big ache that no longer differentiates one pain from another. Coal made me eat after we trained, watching to make sure I swallowed every spoonful of beef stew without falling asleep in the bowl. And now that I can finally lie down, there is the damn wolf.

Not only is he on my bed, but he is splayed out to his fullest —including sticking out all four legs, his tail, and even a lolling tongue to maximize his claim of the real estate. The wolf lifts a sleepy muzzle from my pillow and opens one yellow eye to watch my arrival before nuzzling right back into the down covers.

"Really, Shade?" I pull off my jacket and toss it onto his sleeping form.

Shade growls in indignation, but I just toss my sweater onto him as well before dropping onto the bed to take off my boots. Stars, my body hurts, especially where bits of stray sand worked themselves into my leathers, leaving my skin raw and bloody underneath.

The mattress shifts behind me, and a wet wolfish nose prods my back. My skin tingles as Shade sniffs my hair then licks the back of my neck with a warm lupine tongue.

"Knowing that you are not really a wolf sheds a new light on this, you know," I tell Shade over my shoulder.

He growls again, this time as if to say, *I am very much a wolf.*

"You are a wolf of convenience," I tell him. "You know I'd kick you out of my bedchamber if you were in your fae form, so here you are, taking advantage of my goose-down mattress while looking too adorable to evict."

There is a quick flash of light and suddenly the wolf is replaced by a black-haired male, his face still close to my neck. He wears what he must have had on when he shifted back to his wolf this evening, which isn't much—a pair of gray woolen trousers that button in two rows high on his abdomen, supple leather boots, and no shirt. Not even the sleeveless open-front vest he wore earlier. "So which is it, cub," he growls into my ear, his wolfish scent giving way to one of fresh earth, damp from rain. "Am I adorable? Or are you going to evict me from your chamber now?"

"How have you and Coal coexisted for the past three hundred years?" I demand. "The only way you could be more different is if one of you were a sclice."

"Coal does have that pig reek, doesn't he?" Shade muses.

I shove his shoulder, though it does little good.

The male chuckles and retreats to stretch out his full fae form, boots and all, on my bed. The bastard takes up no less space this way, with his hands crossed behind his head and his yellow eyes watching me intently.

I swallow.

Shade's wolf is adorable—but Shade is beautiful. Golden skin, velvety and rippling with latent muscles even when relaxed, hard biceps framing his face. Strong, confident cheekbones. A piercing yellow gaze that makes my heart race despite my bone-aching fatigue.

Shade's nose twitches and his eyes cloud with concern. "I smell blood."

"Raw skin." I frown at him. "Does it bother you? I mean, does it make your wolf want to maul me or something—like sensing weak prey?"

Shade considers me for several heartbeats. "You aren't prey," he says finally. "You could never be prey. But yes, smelling blood on you bothers us. We don't enjoy seeing you hurt."

Clearly, Shade didn't watch Coal in action. "I'm fine," I lie.

He rolls lazily onto one elbow. "Prove it."

"Prove what?" I cross my arms, smelling a rat. "More importantly, how."

A shamelessly wolfish grin. "By taking your clothes off."

The demand rushes through me, settling somewhere between my legs. I cross my thighs and point at the door. "Scram, wolf fiend."

Shade makes a swipe for me, pulling back when I smack his wrist. "How about a compromise? Just your shirt."

My brows pull together in memory of what Tye tried— and failed—to accomplish earlier. "Are you all in on this 'don't take Lera's word about her body' scheme?"

A flush of color touches Shade's cheeks and ears, their points peeking out from shaggy hair. He studies me from under his lashes for a moment longer. Then the bastard pounces.

One moment I'm sitting on the edge of my bed, and the next he's pulled me all the way onto the mattress while he kneels beside me, his arms shamelessly around my hips— which does little to smother the heat kindling there. "I'll make it worth your while," Shade promises, his lips at the base of my neck, right over my quickening pulse.

"Please don't rip my shirt like Tye did in the stream," I say, closing my eyes in an attempt to calm my rebellious body. "I rather like this—"

The *this* is over my head and off me in a heartbeat, Shade's calloused palm brushing down the groove of my spine, wiping away stray grains of sand from my bruises and cuts.

I shudder.

Shade's hand on my hip tightens, pinning me in place against his hard, warm body. "The mortal world dampens my magic," he says into my ear, his voice soothing even as his probing fingers give no quarter. "But I'll heal this once we are in Lunos. And we'll make sure no one leaves these on you again." Shade touches one of the marks from Zake's belt, his soft voice laced with violence.

I glance over my shoulder and snort. "As those account for about one tenth of my current bruises, that's hardly reassuring."

Shade flinches.

"No," I twist toward him, coming up to my knees. Apparently, I like him flinching as little as he tolerated me shuddering. "It was a jest," I say, my hand reaching up to brush Shade's hair from his face. The lock is shiny and softer than I expected, springing right back into place the moment I release it.

Shade's neck bobs and he catches my wrist, the few inches of air between us suddenly thick. Crackling. His mouth opens slightly, the elongated canines near and sharp and glistening with danger. My chest tightens, my breath suddenly gone from my lungs.

"You . . . have long lashes," I say, leaning closer. "Girls would kill for those."

"I have many long things," Shade breathes, his hand cupping the back of my head, tangling in my hair. "Patience, it seems, is not one of them."

I open my lips to respond, only to find Shade's mouth covering mine, his lips soft and warm enough to heat a whole palace. My own mouth yields in answer, and Shade's kiss deepens, the hand in my hair tightening until my whole scalp tingles. Sings. *Stars.*

Shade pulls away slowly, his canines gently scraping my lower lip as I moan softly into him.

My heart pounds, the warmth between my legs a downright flame, and I try to catch my breath. "Did you plan that?" I demand.

Shade grins, makes a noncommittal sound, and turns back into his wolf, demonstratively making a circle on my bed before curling up with his tail over his nose. His body manages to press against my back, his rhythmic breathing soothing and steady.

"Why do you do that?" I ask when I can speak again. "Stay in your wolf form so much?"

No answer.

"Being a wolf to avoid talking to me while lounging around on my bedding is a dirty, cowardly trick."

Shade snorts, buries his head deeper beneath his paws, and settles into a calm sleep punctuated by soft snores that turn into whimpers when I shift out of reach. Frowning, I move closer, resting my hand on the sleeping wolf's flank. The whimpering stops, the rhythmic rise of his chest and his twitching eyelids speaking of a dream-filled slumber.

16

LERALYNN

"We'll cross Mystwood this morning," River announces as the five of us gather around a wooden table in the empty common room. The inn's servants cleaned my clothes overnight, leaving them outside my door without giving me a chance to thank them. I think everyone at the inn wants us gone, despite the amount of coin River has been placing in the innkeeper's palm.

The males nod to the commander while I struggle to keep my relief in check, the plan to leave effectively saving me from another training session with Coal.

The blond warrior's amused grin tells me he's read my thoughts regardless.

I give Coal a vulgar gesture and River cocks a brow at the two of us.

"I'll get the horses ready," says Coal, pushing himself away from the table. Shade and Tye join him.

I shift in my seat. River hasn't done or said anything to warrant my nerves, and yet his very presence singes the air.

Perhaps it's the unyieldingly vigilant gray gaze betraying an always-working mind. Or maybe it's the quieter way the others act around him, as if feeling the need to behave in their commander's presence.

River turns to me, his back straight. Today, he is dressed in a burnt-red coat, the high collar crisp and the buttons polished to a shine, and black pants that cover equally black boots. "Are you all right, Leralynn?" His voice is deep and strong, a voice more used to ordering than asking.

"Yes. Very. I mean, yes." I get to my feet, River's muscular arm reaching around to smoothly pull my chair away. "Where are we going, exactly?"

River rises, offering me his arm to lead me outside. The gesture would be absurd from anyone else, but River somehow makes it look both natural and dignified. "Across Mystwood and into Slait Court to rest and resupply before crossing into the neutral lands. The latter will be the most difficult part of the journey to the Citadel."

His words are even, but I sense there is something he's not saying. I frown back at the inn. "Don't we need the Slait king's permission to enter?"

"It's been arranged." River's jaw tenses. "The Slait king is absent just now. He will be busy for several days yet."

"You know him?"

"Yes." River's eyes darken and he opens the door, avoiding my gaze.

Something in my chest stirs, the same way it did when River and I tangled yesterday. So instead of keeping my mouth shut like a wise person, I turn to study the commander. "You don't like him very much?"

"He doesn't like me very much," River snaps, dropping my arm.

I step back, my heart pounding.

River stalks to his horse, swinging himself into the waiting saddle. For a stupid moment, all I can think about is how River's muscled body might feel behind me in the saddle, his strong thighs pressed against my legs. The moment passes and I frown at the males. Coal and Tye are mounted already, and Shade is in his wolf form, his tail swishing smoothly back and forth. Which leaves me standing on the ground alone.

River runs his hand over his face. "Forgive me, Leralynn. Will you do me the honor of riding with me?"

No. "Of course," my treacherous voice says, and River pulls me easily into the saddle before him, satisfying my earlier curiosity: Sharing a saddle with River feels like leaning against a heated boulder. I breathe deep, inhaling his scent. Woodsy and strong as an oak tree.

Plainly, I've already been around the fae males too long if the first thing I do is smell them.

"Your seat is nice," River says behind me.

"Excuse me?"

"Your seat." He clears his throat, and I can feel his sudden flush of heat. "The way you sit atop a horse. It's better than it was two days ago."

"Oh." It's my turn to trip over my words. "Right. There was a great deal of falling in the past two days."

"I know." River's arms tighten around me, though I can't tell whether the gesture is out of concern or simple utility. "If it's any consolation," he adds quietly, leaning down to speak in my ear, "Coal would do the same to any one of us." River surveys the group. "Let's move."

The horses move out at a gentle canter that feels heavenly after Coal's lunge-line drills, and after a few minutes I relax back against River's muscled body. I feel his hitch of breath and wonder if I've made him uncomfortable, but before I can move away, his arm grows even tighter around my waist. Mystwood rises in front of us, a dense green wall ringing with birdsong.

"How are we crossing through Mystwood with sclices and all?" I ask, looking at the approaching trees. "For that matter, how did you all cross it to get here? I thought the point of these woods was to prevent tourism."

"Tourism?" A soft laugh rumbles through River's chest. "Sclices are just invasive parasites, and it would be poor manners to leave them roaming so near Mystwood's mortal border. To cross the true wards in the heart of the forest, a passage key is required." I feel River shifting behind me and turn to find him pulling something out of his shirt, a disk hanging around his neck on a leather thong. "When it became clear that our fifth was in the mortal lands, the Citadel's Elders Council granted me one of these. We will use it to traverse back the same way we came. For all intents and purposes, it will make us invisible to Mystwood."

"Useful," I mutter. "Are there many of these passage keys?"

"No." River raises his voice to speak to the rest of the quint. "Remember that the key will only cover a ten-pace circle, so keep close and control the horses. Shade won't be able to give us distance. Leralynn, take a deep breath."

I don't have a chance to ask what is about to happen before we take another step and the air ripples around us, settling again into the same forest. Except it isn't the same forest. The great ash trees rising to the sky still stand, but the smaller branches are gone from sight. The greens, yellows, and reds of the autumn foliage are dull and gray; the sweet smell of sap is nothing but a thin shadow of itself. Even the sun somehow fails to shine onto the trail despite a clear sky.

"Why is everything so . . ." I search for the right word, "faded?" That is as close a description as I can think of, though it still falls short. Faded things still exist, and half of what should be here is somehow missing.

"We've stepped into the Gloom." River's voice ruffles my hair. His, but lacking some of its rich undertones. "The world hasn't faded; you are simply seeing a shadow of it."

"I don't understand."

"Imagine the normal world—what we call the Light—as a cloak," River explains patiently. "The Gloom is the cloak's inside lining, moving and shifting along with the main cloth but separate from it as well. Some of the stitching, like the ash trees you see, penetrates all the way through. Other pieces are shallower, existing only in the Light without roots here."

"Why are we here?" I ask, shivering. It's cold. The kind of cold that a warm cloak won't fix.

"Mystwood is warded. The key allows us to pass as long as we move through the Gloom, and it makes us invisible to the beings that dwell here. You are safe." River's voice is certain and calm, as if nothing like magic or nature would dare contradict him. "Distance changes here too. What would be a two-day ride in the Light will take us less than six hours here."

Six hours. I bite my lip. "Does the Gloom exist in the mortal world?" I don't say home. These past few days with the males have felt more like home than Zake's estate ever did.

"Yes, but the barrier between Light and Gloom is impenetrable in the mortal lands," says River, oblivious to the effect his deep, gravelly voice is having on me. "You will sometimes see shadows of things that dwell here, dark things that mortals explain away as odd tricks of light."

Movement at the corners of my eyes catches my attention, and it's all I can do not to shudder and curl myself into River's body. "The Gloom seems an efficient way to travel," I say, trying to make my voice light and failing.

"It isn't. Most fae never step foot in the Gloom, and those who do just use the few shortcut passages they've forged. Without a key, it's too dangerous here. Even without the local residents, the Gloom itself feeds on you. Stay too long or go too deep, and you may never leave. I called the Gloom a lining to the normal world, but it's a living lining, with currents and depths and shallows like the ocean."

My bravery chooses that moment to utterly fail, blood draining from my face as my hands tremble in their grip on the horse's mane. Of course. Of course I'd shatter when it's River sitting beside me—River, who probably feeds on fear like the bloody Gloom feeds on life. I can almost hear the commander's thoughts. *Weak, small, useless human.*

River switches his reins to one hand, his other settling on my right shoulder. The large, heavy palm cups my entire joint. River says nothing, his silent breath even and steady against the top of my head. Despite the lack of words, strength from River's sheer confidence drapes over me, a blanket of safety against the Gloom's murmuring shadows.

"How do you know so much about the Gloom if most fae never step here?" I ask finally, as much to hear River speak as to assure myself that my own voice still functions.

River stays silent for several moments longer. "Because we are not most fae," he says, his voice hard. Unyielding. "We are a quint, warriors of the Citadel. Our main duty is to protect Lunos from the things that dwell here." He releases a breath. "We are not safe for you, Leralynn. We aren't safe for any mortal."

17

LERALYNN

*D*espite the promised safety of the key, River moves us as quickly as the horses allow, and his body doesn't truly relax until we pass Mystwood's shore and emerge from the Gloom into the sun-filled world once more.

I gasp as my lungs draw their fill of Lunos, the air tasting like the richest of wines. Behind me, Mystwood's trees once more stand in their gowns of greens and yellows, the occasional bright-red maple leaves floating down like butterflies. We appear to be standing in the countryside, fields of wheat extending in all directions, broken by the outline of a deep-blue lake. Far ahead, a range of breathtaking white-capped mountains rises toward the clouds.

Chip chirip.

I twist around, the sound of a bird's call a balm to my nerves after hours in the Gloom. Perfect. Like everything in this realm.

Chip Chirip.

Tye dismounts and River lowers me into the other male's waiting arms. Tye cradles me against his chest for a moment, and I shamelessly burrow my face into his neck, savoring the pine-and-citrus smell. "Is this Slait?" I ask as Tye finally settles me onto the ground. "Are you sure we're allowed to be here? It would be a shame if some overzealous archers shot something pointy through us for trespassing right when we came up for air."

Tye frowns at River.

"We are fine," the commander says. He busies himself with taking the saddle off his horse to let the animal rest. "It's been . . . arranged."

There it is again, a hesitation. Something River isn't telling me.

"River isn't telling many people many things," Tye says lightly, and I realize I said my thought out loud. "And if you find that quality as annoying as I do, then I suggest you give up interacting with Coal altogether too."

I narrow my eyes at the redheaded male. "You don't seem worried about patrols either."

Tye grins, his white teeth flashing. "I am always worried about patrols, Lilac Girl." His grin widens. "I'm just certain that none of them will want to shoot me from afar and deny themselves the pleasure of dragging me to some dungeon or another. Now, more importantly, tell me how you feel?"

"Alive," I say honestly. "More alive than I've ever felt. As if the world has become more potent. Juicer. Is that an aftereffect of stepping into the Gloom? Or is Lunos different from the mortal realm?"

"You can feel Lunos's magic, then," Coal says behind me.

"Interesting." Tye cocks a brow, his gaze roaming

arrogantly over me. "I do wonder if Lunos will enhance your *other* senses as well."

I roll my eyes and shove Tye, succeeding only in pushing myself onto my ass. I stand, dusting myself off with as much dignity as I can reclaim. "Can someone please tell me why you are all so sure that some patrol isn't about to descend on us," I say.

"We have one of the Citadel's keys," says River, his back to me still. "We've been tracked the entire time. Everyone of importance knows exactly where we are."

"Especially Autumn," says Tye, his words aimed at River's back and pregnant with meaning. "How long until she—" Tye cuts off just as a small, gorgeous female steps out from thin air, squeals, and launches herself at River. She chuckles as River utters an *oomph* on impact.

"You're back!" the female—who I presume must be Autumn—declares, her many blond braids swinging from a perfectly shaped head. She wears bright-green silk trousers that sway sensually with each move of her hips and a cropped top that would be scandalous in my world but looks natural on her. Autumn twists around, her gray eyes sparkling when they fall on Shade, who's flashed into his fae form. "Stars take me, Shey-Shey, you are *back*, back?"

A pang of jealousy that I've no right to sours my stomach as Shade opens his arms to welcome Autumn into an embrace. Of course the males have lives and friends and . . . and lovers.

I swallow and am taking a step back to give the reunion some privacy when the female's eyes finally land on me—land and widen in unabashed delight.

"You are the fifth?" Slender arms that are much stronger than they look wrap me in a rib-crushing embrace, releasing me only when I make a pitiful choking sound. "Sorry." The female cringes sheepishly. "You're human, right?"

"Very much so," I say, rubbing my ribs.

Autumn loops her arm through mine, and I'm starting to wonder whether the female is truly fae or some natural force given flesh.

"My brother better be thanking the bloody stars," Autumn says, shooting River a squint that would do a schoolmarm proud. "In fact, all these animals better be nice to you, or I'm going to rip their pointed little ears right off their empty heads and feed them to the hounds. Or the pigs. The pigs are not nearly as picky about their food."

"They've been good," I assure her quickly. "I think they can keep their ears for another day at least."

She laughs, the sound musical and infectious, and starts drawing me away. "I'm Autumn, by the way. Why don't we go on ahead. You won't believe how dull it gets without a female around, and I want to know all about you."

"Autumn," River's low voice rumbles in our wake.

The female waves a hand over her shoulder. "Take care of the beasts like a good lad, River. I can already see that you've brought no clothes for your fifth, and I'm getting that corrected right now."

As Autumn pulls me away, a small, displeased growl sounds behind us. I turn my head to find all four males in a line, prowling closer on instinct. Predators protecting their kill.

Instead of blanching, Autumn puts her hands on her slender hips and manages to stare down at all four males from her much lower height. "You four can simmer more quietly and find the manners that appear to have fallen from your pockets. The females wish to talk, and we will see you at dinner." Her nose crinkles. "You lot better bathe before then too. Coal especially—you reek of sclice blood and frustration."

I have no chance to say anything before the world darkens and I'm pulled through thick-as-pudding nothingness into a sunbathed bedroom with dresses, weapons, and jewelry scattered over every surface.

18

LERALYNN

"What was that?" I ask, finding my voice.

Autumn grins like a fiend. "A shortcut. One of the folds in the Gloom. River and I invested a great deal of our childhood into ferreting ways out of this damn house. To call Father a paranoid power-hungry bastard is such an understatement, it renders the whole phrase meaningless." Autumn hops onto her bed, letting her legs swing down. Now that I look closer, I can see the resemblance to River more clearly, from the gray eyes to the high, perfectly aligned cheekbones. What Autumn lacks in size, she makes up for in unabashed enthusiasm for . . . everything, it seems. "So? Tell me all."

I look around for a place to sit. Everything in this room costs many times what I'm worth in the mortal world as an indentured servant, from the intricately carved four-poster bed to the diamond earring tossed atop a pair of discarded stockings. Four tall, arched windows span the far wall, letting in dazzling sunlight that glances off the rich green-gold carpet and silks draping off seemingly every surface. Finally spotting a stool with only a single priceless silk dress on it, I move the garment gently and sit down.

My mind scrolls through words in search of something to make me sound less pathetic, comes up empty, and settles on the plain truth. "I'm Leralynn—Lera—and until two days ago, I was an indentured servant on an estate near Mystwood. Then whatever magic creates quints made a mistake and accidentally bonded me with River, Shade, Tye, and Coal. Now we are headed to the Citadel to sever the tether so the males can have someone more suitable. So you won't need to put up with me for too long."

Autumn's face darkens at my words, her gray eyes flashing with a sudden fury to match River's. "A mistake? Sever the tether? I *will* feed River's ears to the pigs." She pauses, her head cocking, listening to sounds my mortal body can't hear. "And there is the culprit now," she announces a moment before I hear a knock. "I warded my rooms," she explains, glaring at the door.

The knock sounds again. Louder. More insistent.

Autumn sighs and waves her hand toward the door, which opens obediently onto a tousled River.

His gaze rushes around the room until it finds me, slowing upon touching my flesh. "Leralynn." His voice is rough, with an undertone of urgency that I understand as little as my chest's sudden tightness. We've been apart for only minutes, yet River's presence is already filling a hole that began festering in our separation. My gaze drinks him in thirstily, the taut planes of his face, the broad daylight-blocking shoulders, the damn stick-straight back. His gray eyes brush mine, and the room heats around us, the air suddenly thick. Crackling. With what seems like physical effort, River breaks his gaze away from me and finds Autumn's face. "I need to—"

Autumn is on her feet before he can finish, one slender finger poking River's wide chest. "How dare you consider breaking Lera from the quint? Have you lost what passed for brains somewhere in Mystwood?"

River's jaw tightens but he grabs Autumn's wrist with careful gentleness. "Can we discuss what battling Mors's trash would do to a mortal female later, please?" he asks. "I need to speak with Leralynn."

"I imagine you had at least six hours to discuss things with Lera," Autumn says, scoring a very good point. "Now it's my turn. And you'll be happy to know that Father is off making someone else's life miserable for a change."

"I didn't imagine you'd bring Leralynn here otherwise," says River.

"Exactly." Autumn makes a shooing motion, but I can see a sharp intelligence beneath the bubbly exterior. "Go occupy yourself and we'll see you for dinner. And if you must fret over something, I suggest wondering why my patrols are reporting that one of the Citadel elders is already at the edge of Slait Court and riding here full speed."

Autumn's patrols?

River shifts his weight, dismissing Autumn's words with a brisk wave of his hand. "I am carrying a Mystwood key; of course they are concerned. If I were an elder, I'd not let it out of my sight for a minute more than I must."

"You are the crown prince of Slait and lead the strongest quint in the whole of Lunos, bar the Elders Council itself, River." Autumn's hard voice resembles nothing of the bubbly girl she was a few minutes earlier. "You think no one was jealous of your power at its height? Secretly glad when Kai's death made you wither? There are many who will little like seeing you complete again."

Except they aren't complete. They have me stuck on like a parasitic growth, I think—just before the rest of Autumn's words penetrate. My head snaps toward River, my eyes widening. "Wait. Prince? You are the crown prince of Slait?"

River's gaze catches mine and then drops to the floor.

Prince. The title echoes in my mind. Not just any immortal fae warrior, River is also the bloody prince of one of the three courts. His words and actions of the past few days reshuffle, clicking into place. The aura of unyielding command, the coin to spare, the certainties about Slait thrown about with no explanation. I knew River was concealing something—I just never imagined it would be this large. This vital. I realize Autumn is still talking only when River shushes her, his attention fully on me.

Commanding gray eyes flinch. Lower.

"River—" Autumn starts.

"Later." The snap of command in River's voice has me on my feet and backing toward the door.

Prince. Prince. Prince. That's what he so carefully didn't tell me. My mouth dries, the words weighing a hundred tons each. "Is this a palace?"

"Yes," says River.

I nod. "And were you always intending to bring us here?"

"No." River runs his fingers through his hair. "I had decided we wouldn't come here at all. Autumn got the jump on me."

I nod again. Slowly. Carefully. River lied. Because he thought he might get away with it. Because he felt he could lie to me. Because lying to a lowborn mortal girl is all right.

"You didn't tell her?" Autumn's hands are fisted at her hips. "Get out of my room, River."

"Leralynn." River extends a hand toward me.

I shake my head and back away, the sudden need to hit something overpowering my thoughts. I don't even care if that something hits back. I know exactly what I need. "Where is Coal?"

"Still on his way here with Tye, Shade, and the horses," River says quietly.

"I'll wait for him in the stable, then." I take a step toward the door. "You have a stable, right?" I ask Autumn. "Or . . . if there are several, just tell me where to go and I'll wait there."

"I'll take you," Autumn offers, moving her slender body between River and me. Slipping her arm through mine, the female guides me out of her room, firmly shutting the door before River can follow. "River can be a thoughtless ass," she tells me as we step into the corridor—which alone shouts to the royalty of this place. The long passage could be a receiving room for its plush green rug, dangling candelabras, and frescoes of fae in love, life, and war decorating the walls.

"Would it be all right if we called on the seamstress first?" Autumn asks. She is just a bit taller than I am, which probably makes her tiny for a fae female, and glides with the same preternatural grace as her brother does.

"I don't need anything," I say quickly. I can't pay for a handkerchief in this place, much less clothing.

Autumn snorts. "You need everything. Moreover, I can guarantee that River is already placing the order, because he probably thinks measurements are a frilly extra." She stops, turning to touch my shoulder, her lower lip caught between her teeth. "I know you've no reason to care about those four, much less risk your life to defend Lunos against Mors's darkness, and I've no right to beg it of you, but . . . please just consider them."

"Has there ever been a quint with a mortal in it?" I ask.

She shakes her head. "*And* there has only ever been one other gender-mixed one—the Elders Council. Most are all male or all female. There is something very special about you, Lera. I know it makes no sense, but I think the quint has been waiting for you for a very long time."

19

LERALYNN

he measurements take half an hour, and I'm waiting at the stable when Coal, Tye, and Shade canter in. Coal's gaze goes to mine mid-stride and he dismounts before the horse is fully stopped, landing a pace away from me.

I open my mouth to make my request, but Coal is already holding a callused hand out to me. "Come, mortal," he says quietly. "I know where to go."

I follow in silence as Coal leads me behind the stables to a sand-filled training yard, where several guards are practicing with wooden blades. The guards' inquisitive stares upon seeing me dissolve into smoke the instant they notice Coal, who simply crosses his arms and surveys the training court. Within a moment the sand is empty, the males bowing low and scattering, even those who were plainly in the middle of a sparring match when we arrived.

"Are you a prince of something too?" I ask, biting the ends of my words.

"I am a warrior of the quint," Coal says shortly. Picking up two small leather targets, Coal straps them onto his hands. "The same as you."

I snort. "The great warrior that is me, yes."

Coal weighs me with his gaze, his face tense. Turning on his heels, he removes the hand targets and takes three practice blades from the rack. Blades in hand, the male strides over to a training post, a larger version of the rope-covered pillar in the inn's paddock. Coal tosses two of the training swords to the sand and swings the third one through the air, his whole body a blur.

The crack of wood as the blade shatters takes my breath.

Discarding the now-useless stick, Coal picks up the next sword, his muscles cording into a smooth arc as he shatters the blade in a single blow. With the third blade, Coal cracks the training pillar itself.

"That's impossible," I whisper, blinking at the debris.

"You make it possible," Coal replies shortly. A gentle wind billows his loose black shirt, the fabric on one side outlining his cut abdominals. "We can only draw full power when the quint is complete." He kicks the wood away. "You may not feel like a great warrior. Yet. But you are essential to our unit as a whole. We cannot function fully without you—nor you without us."

I take this in silently, anger still sizzling in my mind.

"But in answer to your first question," Coal continues, "no, River is the only royal among us. And yes, he should have told you earlier."

"He isn't the only one who can speak," I snap. The words escape before I can catch them, but Coal doesn't flinch.

"It was his story to tell, not ours." Reclaiming the leather targets, Coal puts them on his hands again and holds them out before me. "Punches. Use what passes for body weight on you."

I need no further invitation. My hands curl desperately into fists and I sink one into a leather pad, the impact echoing through my arm and making my knuckles sing. I strike again. Again. As if my fists can erase the lies, can reclaim my shreds of dignity.

Weak. Lowborn. Mortal. I punch the pad with each stinging thought.

The fae warrior towering before me starts moving, making me dance for the pleasure of striking the pad, until my breath comes in short gasps and sweat beads at the roots of my stupidly thick hair. His blue eyes glow, his beautiful face placid but for a small smile at the corners of his lips.

River is a prince and I am peasant muck. He never wanted me to step foot in his palace. I was to be his dirty little secret until the Citadel corrected the magic's mistake.

Strike. Strike. Strike. My knuckles bleed as I pound them into the pads. The sweat coating my skin now soaks my hair, running in thick drops down my face. *Strike. Duck. Turn.* Whatever I do, however I move or hit, Coal has a new target waiting for me each time.

I am not a toy, my mind suddenly shouts at the pads, my bloody fists slamming into the leather. *I am not a pet. Lying to me isn't all right.* Another punch, this one jolting my shoulder and sending a branch of pain through my arm. *I . . .* Bile rises up my throat. Because this isn't just about the lies. It's worse. It's about the truth.

I slam both my hands into the targets at the same time, not caring how ineffective it is, because the dark fear inside my chest is now tumbling out, forcing itself into words. "I don't belong," I shout at the bloodied leather. "Not here. Not anywhere. I. Don't. Belong."

"I know," says Coal, and I realize the pads are gone from

his hands, his palms clamping hard around my fists. "I don't either. But here we both are."

I stare at the male, my chest heaving with gasping breaths. Tiny drops of blood escape our desperate grip. His pale eyes' purple tinge shines in the setting sun, the muscles of his square jaw so tight they tremble. His scent is musky and male and harsh like steel.

My vision blurs, the stinging in my eyes betraying tears. I want to turn my head, but Coal's gaze won't let me move. No pity. There is never pity in Coal's eyes. But something more. Deeper.

Coal's face hovers above me, so close I can feel him inhale my scent. Feel the warm tickle of air when he releases his breath. His mouth is stern, his lips holding the promise of velvet. Coal lowers our joined hands, stretching my fists to my sides.

"But here we both are," I whisper, echoing him.

"Yes." He swallows and steps back sharply, releasing his grip on me as if suddenly realizing he held molten steel. His voice is rough when he speaks again. Commanding. "Come," he says, jerking his chin toward a small wooden shack at the sand's edge.

Following Coal inside, I find a wooden table and several benches, all surrounded by racks and walls covered with training equipment and glinting steel. The air smells of sharpening stones, sweat, and sand. Leaving me to drop gracelessly onto a bench, Coal steps away to rummage through a trunk by the far wall.

I can't help watching him. The way each movement is precise and flowing, the way muscle shifts beneath his shirt, the way he crouches smoothly to open the heavy lid. A panther. Gorgeous and dangerous. Deadly. There is no hesitation in anything Coal does either. Not when he walked us onto the sand; not now, when he's rummaging around in an old trunk. I wonder whether he knows the palace as well as he knows this training ground. And then I'm certain I know the answer.

Coal returns with a small box, removing bandages and a pungent green salve from inside. "You are angry at River for not telling you he is the Slait crown prince, yes," Coal says quietly, leaning muscled forearms against the table. "But you are *angrier* because you think we all led you on, dangling an invitation to a group you can never be part of. Peasant, slave, indentured servant—whatever you call yourself, you don't belong among royals and you know it. You aren't good enough. You never can be."

Each of Coal's words pierces my soul, striking its target truer than my fists ever did. "Are you going to claim that none of that is true?" I say, a challenge in my voice.

Coal's eyes hold mine with infuriating, icy calm. "I won't. I'm not in the habit of wasting my breath." Reaching across the table, he draws my left hand toward him. My hand looks absurdly small in his palm, his thumb and forefinger capable of encircling my whole arm. Taking the edge of a bandage, Coal gently dabs the blood from my skinned knuckles, examining the cuts beneath. "You have to discover the truth for yourself, mortal. You won't believe it otherwise. Not truly."

Reaching into the salve, Coal smears a small glob of it onto my knuckles. The damn goop stings as horridly as it smells, and I hiss, jerking my arm away.

Coal tightens his grip. "Next time, wrap your hands first and strike with your first two knuckles here." He traces a gentle finger across the tops of my fingers, making me shiver.

"A bit late for the sage advice," I say through clenched teeth, reluctantly letting him take hold of my second arm.

Coal's gaze flickers up to me. "Like I said, I don't like to waste my breath. You weren't ready to hear it earlier. You needed to hit the pads first." Finishing with the cuts, Coal wraps a clean cloth around my knuckles, paying more attention than necessary to tucking in the stray ends. "I can't draw the sting away," he says, his voice aimed at the bandage. "But I am very familiar with the sensation."

I swallow, my heart pounding as my free hand reaches forward to touch Coal's forearm. River is from Slait. Tye from Blaze. Shade and Kai from Flurry. "What court are you from, Coal?" I ask, hoping he'll answer me this time.

Coal tenses, his eyes now on the tabletop. "I'm not," he says quietly. "I'm from Mors."

LERALYNN

I'm from Mors. Coal's words echo in my head as a servant, who introduces herself as Mika, ushers me from the training yard to a palace room that she says has been assigned to me. My eyes trail the now-familiar frescoes and candelabras to a door beside Autumn's own suite. "This can't be right," I tell Mika. "The royals' rooms are here."

"I'm quite certain," the female replies, her voice light and musical. "Prince River had an order of clothes sent here for you, and then Princess Autumn had that order cancelled and reordered in different sizes. And then the prince had a bathtub and hot water brought in, but Master Shade refused to move from where the tub was supposed to go, and it took some time to make other arrangements for it."

I wince. "I'm so sorry for all the trouble."

"Don't you dare be sorry," Mika says, holding the door open for me. "It's been a very long time since we saw River fuss over a female. It's . . . it's a better homecoming than we've had in centuries."

"River isn't fussing—" I cut off as my room's sweeping ceiling spins my world. The chamber is even grander than Autumn's, if that's possible, though it's more likely that actually being able to see the floor skews my perception. The bed, large enough to sleep a family of seven, is covered with an airy sky-blue duvet, while matching silk curtains frame the floor-to-ceiling windows and a dangling candelabra bathes the room in starlight. A small dais in the other corner of the room holds . . .

"Out, Shade!" I yell at the wolf lounging on a platform plainly designed for the tub, which now sits on the plush rug instead. "You can't possibly even be comfortable up there, and there's no chance in hell that I'm bathing with you watching, be you wolf or worm."

The wolf rises lazily, making sure to take his time stretching each and every limb before stepping down. For a lightning-quick predator, the furry beast can be slow as molasses. Finally, with all four paws on the rug, Shade lifts his tail into the air and demonstratively trots past Mika and me into the corridor.

"Sorry about that," I tell Mika. "Shade's wolf has worse manners than a soup-bound hen." I say this part loudly enough to reach into the corridor, and I grin at the echoing growl.

"Let's get you bathed for dinner, my lady," the fae female says, as if evicting wolves from sleeping chambers were an everyday occurrence and not meant to distract one from more important tasks. Opening up the armoire, Mika removes a flowing dress of red silk, with luscious skirts and a tight bodice that ties in the back, leaving the shoulders bare. "I think the red dress here might suit you best for tonight. Might you step into the tub?"

Three quarters of an hour later, Mika has tousled me into the ruby-red dress, cleverly clipping flowing silk to my wrists, which makes the garment appear to have wings. The light material cascades off my hips, except for a slit along one thigh that should make me feel exposed but is tastefully sensual instead. Coal's hard work on the bandages has been abandoned, and my untamable auburn hair has been braided on one side and left loose on the other so it cascades over my shoulder like a shining waterfall.

I twist tentatively before the mirror. "Stars," I breathe finally, blinking at the flowing cloth, which manages to accent both the curves of my hips and the round swells of my breasts. "I've never worn anything this perfect." I almost don't recognize my face either, with black kohl accentuating my eyes and a light red paint making my lips look soft and full.

"It does suit you well," River says from the doorway. The male is dressed in black flowing pants that taper to wrap snugly around his taut waist. His cream shirt is simple but perfectly tailored, with an open V collar that shows his muscled chest.

My pulse stutters and I have to remind myself that I'm still angry with him.

River's gray eyes flow over the folds of my gown, grazing the bend of my hips and chest. The gaze stops for a heartbeat on my mouth before finally slipping to my eyes, his own widening. For a moment, his face almost looks pained, but then it clears just as quickly.

"Is something wrong?" I ask.

"Everything." River's voice is husky, and he shakes himself in a way that makes me think of Shade. Stars. The quint brothers are so different and yet perfectly connected. Matching. River's hand dips into his pocket, pulling out a gold chain with a jeweled flower pendant weighing down the precious metal. "I thought it might go well with the dress," River says quietly.

"I thought another female would go with the dress even better," I say, returning River's gaze with a raised eyebrow. "Someone royal. Or at least noble."

River swallows, raises his chin. "I deserved that." He stares uncomfortably at the priceless chain, then lays it with care on my dresser. "If you ever change your mind, it will be here," he says and bows formally over his arm. "For now, may I have the pleasure of escorting you to dinner?"

My stomach tightens. I thought I could do this, but now, seeing River as the prince he is . . . "I don't know how to do this, River," I say, stepping back from him. "If you wanted me to bow or curtsy or whatever it is nobles here do, you could have explained it earlier."

"I don't want you to do anything but be you, Leralynn." River steps forward, catching my elbows in his hands. His voice is low. Confident. "We could toss the entire dinner into a basket, spread a blanket in the hayloft, and eat there if you'd like. Autumn might be a bit annoyed if her chocolate cake gets smashed, but we'll be careful with that part. These clothes, the jewels, they are for pleasure, not pressure. Stars, we'll be fortunate if Coal even changes out of his riding leathers for dinner—and remember that for the past ten years, Shade has taken his meals from a dish on the floor."

The corners of my mouth twitch in spite of myself. "I wouldn't dare risk Autumn's chocolate cake," I say, smoothing my hands over the dress. I am not going to wear River's jewels, but this dinner is about all of us.

He exhales. "No hayloft, then?"

"The dining room will be fine," I say, biting my lip. "I don't think this dress fits the stable's atmosphere."

"It doesn't." River's voice is slightly raspy, the air between us suddenly too hot. His eyes simmer with unspent tension, making me wonder what it would be like if he ever let it spill over. "The dress fits you. And you fit any room you are in."

A heartbeat of silence stretches between us before River swallows and steps away, offering me his arm. I take it this time, following him out of the room.

"So this is where you grew up?" I say as we step into the carpeted corridor.

River slows his stride, accepting my unspoken proposal. I talk to him again . . . if he serves up information. "Yes." He looks around at the frescoes. "It was a happy place once, when my mother was alive. My father has always found the notion of offspring unappealing, so with her gone, it did not go well. When the magic chose me to lead the quint, Autumn went to the Citadel with us. Helped the five of us through the training. Don't let her smiles fool you—Autumn is the smartest being in Slait. Once we passed the trials, she returned here and took charge of protecting Slait Court from Mors attack. All the patrols in Slait's Gloom answer to her."

"Not to your father?" I ask.

River's voice is distant. "The king of Slait is of the opinion that Mors attacks are rare enough that the losses are acceptable."

My breath catches. "Your mother—"

"Yes." The answer is so clipped with pain that I can't bear to push him more, and we make the rest of the walk in thoughtful silence. Coal. River. Shade. I wonder if there is a darkness in Tye's past as well. If perhaps more than magic connects us all.

The other three males stand as we enter the dining hall, which has dizzyingly vaulted ceilings lined with what looks like a hundred crystal chandeliers. I think the gesture is a salute to Prince River—until I realize their gazes are locked not on the male, but on me. My skin tingles.

"Stars," Tye says, adding a whistle for emphasis, "how have you managed to hide that from us for days?"

Coal elbows Tye in the ribs, hard enough to make the male grunt in pain. River was right about Coal, I note—the male is wearing black leather pants and the same black shirt he wore during our training. His callused hands look washed and his blond hair looks clean, but it's still tied back tightly.

Shade, in his fae form, walks toward me. He is wearing real clothes for once, a soft cashmere sweater, the same dark gray as his wolf's fur, thin suede pants in a light gray, and supple ankle-high boots. River slides behind me with his palms on the crest of my hips to make room for his quint brother. Shade's large hands brush over my skinned knuckles. "Let's fix that," he says, his yellow eyes brushing mine with a gentleness to match his fingers, and my torn knuckles prickle with heat.

I gasp as the heat peaks and settles like thick wax, leaving fresh pink skin in its wake. "What was that?"

"Healing magic," says Autumn, shifting over on the long bench to make room for me beside her. Like me, Autumn wears a flowing silk gown, though hers is in silvery blue tones. Like me, she also wears a complementary sash of silk to match her dress, but hers is tied around her neck and flowing down her back, mingling with her silver-blond braids. "Would you all let Lera sit down and eat? Maybe ogle her discreetly from across the table?" The males disperse quickly and Autumn grins at me, laying a thick smoky steak on my plate while River adds a salad of ripe tomatoes and crispy lettuce to keep the meat company.

I run my fingers over my freshly healed knuckles.

"I couldn't reach my healing gift in the mortal lands or Mystwood," Shade says softly. "I did try, cub. In both my forms."

Autumn sets down her fork. "Shade shifted form in the mortal lands? That shouldn't be possible. Then again, with the magic choosing Lera, the definition of *possible* has gained some flexibility."

"Speaking of healing," I say carefully, "if anyone else has special powers, it would be nice to know." I think about the earth shaking when the males rode in to fight off the sclices, knowing that River caused it but not exactly how. I wait patiently for someone to tell me the truth.

"Besides the power that comes when a quint physically connects," says Autumn, using her fork to point at the males, "River's magic has a natural earth affinity, which means he can manipulate earth and rock most easily. Shade shifts, with a side of healing. Coal kills things very efficiently, and Tye is just a pain in the ass."

"Anytime you want to go fire to fire, I'm ready, Sparkle," Tye tells the female before turning his head sharply toward me. "Both of us have a magical flame affinity, but my superiority makes River's little sister feel inadequate."

Autumn rolls her eyes. "Magic is a bit like muscle," she tells me. "We all have it, but some of us can only use it to smash things and others of us can use it to write. You can work out for yourself who's who. Oh, and that bastard also shifts. The shift does shut him up nicely, but unfortunately it is better for all of us if he stays fae."

Tye wiggles his brows. "Is that a challenge?"

"What do you shift into?" I ask.

"Don't get him started," River says.

Shade growls. "If you are so determined to show your true colors, Tye, why don't you tell our cub what you were doing when the quint call came."

For the first time since I met the male, I see Tye blush. "I was . . . occupied."

"He was in prison," Shade supplies helpfully.

"Like I said." Tye crosses his arms. "Occupied."

Shade snorts. "The Citadel had to interfere to get that bastard out. And then all five of us went through extra hell just to——"

"I'm hungry," Tye says, breaking off a piece of crusty bread that fills the air with its yeasty aroma. "The overgrown rug over there is altogether too chatty after a decade in wolf form, and I do not see that as a good reason to let dinner go cold."

I lean toward Shade. Information is flowing like wine this evening, and I'm determined to milk it for every last drop. "So what did you mean about going through extra misery on Tye's account?"

"Really, lass?" Tye says between mouthfuls. "Of all the exciting things you could ask about me, that's what you want to know?"

Autumn snorts. "Don't bother asking this lot for a straight story," the princess tells me. "It varies with each bout of masculinity poisoning that these roosters suffer from. Here is the basic——"

"You do remember that I'm your future lord, don't you?" River says sharply.

"Not if being an ass kills you first," Autumn answers

sweetly. Not a rejection of River's status, but not subservience either. Just . . . love. Family. Friendship. And it isn't just Autumn and River, but all of them. I'm just swallowing my envy when Autumn turns back to me, a self-satisfied grin on her face. "All right, then. So the problem with quints is that they are bloody powerful things, and the sudden influx of magic unfortunately doesn't come with a sudden influx of brains."

River glares at her, but the other three chuckle into their cups. Even Coal turns away with a sudden cough.

"The Citadel, which has a realm to protect, needs to somehow rein in these monsters before they piss on the good rug," Autumn continues, undeterred. "Teach them how to work together, test their skills—"

"Instill fear of the Citadel into the quint's souls," River adds darkly, piling more meat and salad onto my quickly emptying plate. "New quints must pass a series of three Citadel trials to be recognized. When a new quint enters the Citadel training grounds, the Elders Council tattoos three runes on each warrior's skin—one for each trial to be passed. The runes keep the initiates confined to the training grounds until the trials are completed. Well, thanks to that red-haired idiot, we had five."

Tye stretches like a cat, spreading his arms wide. "It built character."

Getting the dynamic of this little gathering, I'm smart enough to turn to Autumn for information. "What did Tye do?" I ask.

"Stole priceless gems from the Blaze palace and attempted to sell them to Flurry."

"They were Flurry's to begin with," Tye protests. "I was just returning them to their rightful owner."

Autumn somehow manages to look down her nose at the male. "For a price."

"You want me to work for free?" Tye adjusts his collar primly. "Lilac Girl, wouldn't you rather know what I can turn into?"

"Of course I would," I say, catching everyone's furious headshaking a moment too late.

Tye's grin widens, and in a flash of light there is an orange tiger swishing its tail at the table. Another flash and Shade's wolf pounces on the smug feline, the table overturning in the pair's wake.

LERALYNN

"Cats and dogs?" I say, bending down to rescue the dishes while Autumn shoos the animals from the room and the remaining males right the fallen table. "Shouldn't they be above such things?"

"They are males," says Autumn. "There is nothing they are above."

"When fae change to animal form, the transformation isn't superficial," River explains. "How much of the fae remains varies with each being. Tye's tiger has almost no fae awareness; that is why he doesn't normally shift."

"Is that why Shade stayed a wolf for so long after Kai's death?" I ask.

"The wolf lives in the now," says Coal quietly. "It was easier to bear the loss."

We refill our plates in silence, the platter of meat having miraculously survived the fall. "So what happens now?" I ask finally, somehow certain that the others know I'm not talking about food. My breath stills, a stupid part of me wondering if perhaps River isn't as eager to cut me out of the quint now. A stupid, vanity-filled wish. As nice as the dinner has been, as warm as it feels, we are still bound for the Citadel. And no matter what else, there is one opinion River has never expressed any ambiguity about: Our bond is temporary and will be severed shortly and permanently.

"Now we wait for that elder that Autumn's patrol spotted riding this way," says River, shooting Autumn a glance for confirmation. "I imagine we have at least until morning."

I'M PLEASANTLY full when I return to my room after dinner— proud of myself for having found the way back on my own— and not the least bit surprised to find Shade already curled up in the middle of my bed. Apparently, the cat and dog have either sorted out their differences or chased each other into opposite corners of the palace.

Dropping myself onto the bed, I start pulling off my shoes, the storm of information still raging through my thoughts. Just days ago, my greatest worries were whether Mimi would snatch me a roll from the kitchen and whether I could stay free of Zake's lust and rancor. Now there are immortals and the Gloom, magic and Mors, the bond I can no longer imagine living without and yet am destined to have broken. I've just finished removing my second slipper and am contemplating whether trying to shove Shade over is worth the effort when a knock at the door precedes Tye swaggering into the room.

"He gets to sleep here?" Tye asks, his green eyes filled with immortal indignation. "How is that fair?"

"It isn't about fair, kitten," I say. "It's about me not being able to move two hundred pounds of wolf."

"Watch and learn," Tye instructs primly, grabbing a

pitcher of water from beside the washbasin and, before I can stop him, dousing Shade with it.

Shade is off the bed in the blink of an eye, growling and shaking himself as the hackles rise on the back of his neck. Unperturbed, Tye stretches himself along my bed in the spot Shade occupied and grins lazily. "Problem one solved, bonny lass," he says with a self-satisfied yawn. "Now, tell us whether River is back in your good graces. He's a miserable prick when he's brooding."

River's brooding? I frown, backing away from Shade, who is still shaking water from his fur. The motion apparently brings me too close to my bed, because suddenly I feel Tye's arms snatch me up from the floor.

Leaning his back against the headboard, Tye pulls me onto his lap and sighs with contentment. "Well, Lilac Girl?" he prods.

"Let me go." I try and fail to wriggle free. "I'm sweaty. I need to bathe."

Tye's nose tickles a spot behind my ear, making my breath grow shallow. "I know," he murmurs. "I like it."

A flash of light has Shade changing back into his fae form, his large yellow eyes still shining with indignation as he pulls off his wet sweater and reclaims a space on my bed. Pressing his wide back against the headboard a few inches from Tye, Shade draws my feet onto his lap. I open my mouth to protest the manhandling, but Shade's thumb presses into the arch of my foot, sending a wave of aching pleasure rippling over my skin.

My eyes widen and the small cocky smile touching the corners of Shade's mouth says he knows exactly what he's doing.

A trap, that's what this is. With the first wave of pleasure calming, I'm ready to plead for more. I wiggle my toes hopefully, my whole foot the size of Shade's wide hand. Stars, is being enormous a requirement for this quint's males?

"River," Tye cues, and Shade halts his touch, holding the next stroke of his fingers hostage pending my answer. "What did that wee bastard do, and would you like us to pommel him for it?"

I wrap my arms around myself. "River didn't do anything," I say honestly. "He is what he is. The immortal crown prince of Slait Court. And I am . . . what I am."

"What you are, cub, is the beating heart of the second most powerful quint in Lunos," Shade says quietly. He speaks less than Tye does, but his voice is rich enough to be its own caress. Shade's fingers move again, somehow digging into the muscle fibers at just the right point to send a second pulse of bliss racing through my body.

My mind empties in spite of itself, a soft moan escaping my lips as I ache from yet another skillful stroke. Stars—and Shade is only rubbing my *feet*. As if having heard my thoughts, Shade slides his hands up my shins, my knees, my thighs—

A soft, rumbling growl vibrates along my back, and Tye's lips brush the sensitive inside of my ear. "Careful with those noises, Lilac Girl," he purrs, the warm air caressing my skin. "The ideas they give me are getting more detailed by the heartbeat."

"His. Fault," I manage to say, pointing an accusing hand at Shade. I've seen attractive men before, but the honed bodies of these males are from another world, all sun-kissed skin and shifting muscle.

Shade chuckles softly, back at my feet now. His fingertips ride the length of my arches from toe to heel and back until I can't help it and release a throaty moan.

Tye's green eyes darken. "I warned you," he says, his mouth shifting to cover mine and swallow the sound. His arms, gentle despite their corded muscle, envelop me, brushing along my bare shoulders before sliding across my dress-hugged abdomen.

I shift, inhaling a lungful of pine and citrus as the pleasure of Tye's lips and Shade's hands slowly overwhelms my body. The fingers brushing my skin send sparks flying through me, kindling a need I've never felt before. Never knew I wanted.

Tye's kiss deepens, his tongue claiming my mouth with powerful, luxurious strokes—but instead of satiating my desire, it feeds the flames.

The need grips me low, tingling and pulsing and calling for attention. My flesh craving something so primal, it refuses my mind's reason entirely.

Shade's hand brushes the inside of my thigh, and my heart speeds with equal parts desire and fear. The flesh beneath Shade's fingers quivers, a gently throbbing heat running up my skin.

Up. And up. And . . . I squirm, my backside tightening for a moment before pressing deeper into Tye's lap.

Tye groans and pulls his mouth back, his sharp teeth catching my bottom lip, the canines trailing dangerously across the tender membrane until I whimper.

Tye shuts his eyes, his body tensing as he draws one deep breath, then another. "Those delicious noises are going to be the end of me, Lilac Girl," he says finally, a shudder running through his body.

"Not. Just. You." There is a strain in Shade's deep voice. He moves suddenly, large hands cupping the crests of my hips and pulling me off Tye's lap until my back is flat on the bed. Shade's arms frame my thighs, his golden gaze searching my face desperately. "I want to taste you," he whispers. Begs.

Taste me? My eyes cut to Tye.

The redhead swallows, his neck bobbing. "He isn't talking about your blood, lass."

"What is he talking about?" I whisper.

Shade slowly pulls me toward the edge of the bed until only my back remains on the mattress. Shifting away my flurry of silk skirts, Shade's fingers grip the thin lace of my underwear, his eyes finding mine as his hands still. Tense and poised.

A wave of heat rolls over my skin, my body arching in answer to Shade's silent request.

The fingers flick, ripping the cloth, baring me to Shade as he lowers to his knees. A soft growl vibrates from his chest, sharp teeth gently caressing the insides of my thighs.

I whimper, my need throbbing, the moisture between my legs growing thick and warm. Dripping.

Shade's arms hold my legs firmly, his tongue now lapping the spot his teeth just explored. Tiny little flicks that move closer, closer to where a furnace inside me is building to a blaze. A sudden nip of tender flesh has me gasping for breath.

My hips undulate. My need screams.

Tye's mouth plunges over mine, his hand caressing my shoulders. Tracing my collarbone to the top of that beautiful red dress and jerking the bodice down to liberate my aching breasts. My nipples, suddenly exposed to the air, harden.

Tye purrs with approval.

Shade blows wickedly over my sex, ruffling the hair and skin.

"Please," I beg, pulling my mouth from Tye's, my voice

desperate. The blaze between my thighs is burning so hot I can't keep still. "Shade. Please."

Shade's hands grip my hips, shackling their movement. "Oh, I'm only getting started, cub," he says, his tongue drawing a line through me. He lifts his face to gaze into my eyes as he licks drops of me from his lips.

Tye uses the moment to brush his own rough tongue over my nipples. Lapping at them like a cat with a milk saucer. The content expression on his face says he knows exactly how each of those little licks brings me closer to the cliff Shade has started me toward.

Shade's mouth descends on me again, this time circling mercilessly around my opening, which pulses in instant response. I gasp. Buck. Twist atop cool silken sheets. Searching for the release that Shade and Tye dangle before me.

"Please. Please. Please." The words spill and trip, the promise of coming pleasure so intense it's painful.

"Almost, cub," Shade promises, the tip of his tongue flickering higher and tighter, climbing toward the apex. "Hold on just a bit longer."

I moan, my head swimming, my body so deep in need that I'm dizzy with it.

Shade's hands slide to cup my backside, his fingers digging into my flesh as his mouth moves more, faster, riding the frantic bucking of my hips until—

"Now, Lilac Girl," Tye commands, his thumbs brushing my nipples as the tip of Shade's tongue torments its target with quick, hard taps. "Come for us."

My every muscle tightens, my thighs quivering as I finally tip over the cliff, the blaze inside me exploding and raining stars.

2 2

LERALYNN

*T*he bed beneath me rises and falls in a steady rhythm as a ray of sunlight tickles me awake. I crack open one eye to find myself sprawled atop Shade, my cheek resting on the male's smooth and powerful chest. I expected Shade's fae form to be furrier, given the wolf, but the taut skin is bare.

Very, very bare.

As is my own.

Given last night's activities . . . My face heats before I can finish the thought. And goes hotter still when my body throbs in delicious memory, wondering without permission what it would feel like to have one of the males inside me. Stars. Cringing, I slither off him, hoping to get beneath the blanket before Shade wakes to find me naked on top of him.

The male's arms tighten around my waist, keeping me right where I am, even as he continues sleeping on his back. I try moving again, this time eliciting a displeased growl. "Where are you going?" Shade murmurs sleepily.

"To me, of course," says Tye.

I yelp, twisting to find the redheaded male sitting on one of the chairs, his arms crossed lazily behind his head. He, at least, is fully dressed, in an orange shirt with a wide cloth sash tied snugly around his hard waist. Tye's eyes rake my naked body, from the crown of my head to the arches of my feet, grinning when I snatch up the blanket. "Did you enjoy last night, lass?"

Yes. Stars, yes. I swallow, my cheeks blazing, the renewed desire to do it again prodding at my thighs. No, not just to do it again. To do more. To feel the sizable length of them . . . I clamp my legs together, very directly *not* answering Tye's inquiry. "What are we doing today?" I ask instead, realizing too late the opening I've just given the smirking bastard.

"I can conjure up an idea or two," says Tye, catching with one hand a pillow I launch at him. "Oh, you meant outside the bedroom?"

If I weren't naked, I'd punch him in the nose. Well, if I weren't naked and he weren't three times my size. I huff, and the mattress shifts behind me as Shade sits, his warm hands running down my arms. "It's River's decision. He and the Elders Council have a complicated relationship."

"Explain, please," I say, gathering the blanket around myself and encountering a new problem. With my clothing still on the floor, I'd need to take the blanket with me to retrieve them—leaving a naked Shade behind. If I leave him the blanket, it will be a naked Lera parading through the room. "And tell me how Coal can be from Mors."

Shade solves my dilemma by climbing out of bed first and stretching, the whole naked length of him on display with unabashed ease. I pry my eyes away—with effort—and go for my clothes, leaving Shade to his own devices.

"Well?" I prod when I realize neither of the males has spoken.

"River is a prince, may one day be king, and is bloody powerful," Shade says, his attention on his breeches. "That alone would be enough for the council to see him as a challenge to their authority. Add to the mix him being an opinionated sort of male, and you have an explosive brew on your hands. As for Coal, his story is his to tell."

Tye nods. "Suffice it to say that for the fae, the magic's quint call is impossible to resist. Coal was . . . on the other side when the magic came, and he was all but dead when we found him."

"I thought the fae all left the dark realm." I frown. "What was Coal doing in Mors to begin with?"

"You are half-right," says Tye. His voice sounds odd without his usual mirth. "Mors needs fae and humans the same way mortals need cattle and horses. Work. Food. Sport. In the uprising a thousand years ago, many fae and humans escaped Mors—enough that the dark realm was weakened for lack of labor and food. Enough to build the wall and set up wards. But enough doesn't mean everyone."

I shudder, suddenly cold despite the toasty room. Behind me, Shade takes a step forward, bracing my blanket-covered shoulders. "You don't have to listen, cub," he says quietly. "If you don't want to."

I swallow. I don't want to. I need to.

Catching my eye, Tye continues. "Mors has been trying to break through the wall and its wards for as long as the wall has stood. To reclaim their escaped beasts. They are forever testing the barrier for weaknesses, and . . . Coal was one of the slaves they used for it."

Slave. Coal's words replay themselves in my mind, their colors changing with each new grain of fact. "So it worked?" I ask. "They sent Coal through, and it worked? Why did the hordes not follow?"

"It only worked because Coal is too bloody stubborn to die," Shade says behind me. "No one fully understands how the quint bond works, but the union gives us power, enhancing our innate abilities outright, and when the quint joins in a *physical* union, it creates a whole new reservoir of power to draw on. When the bonding call goes out, it's like nothing else known. Coal was the last one chosen, our fifth, and I think the magic borrowed our life force and strength to let him join us. That isn't something the bastards in Mors can replicate, thank the stars."

I swallow, pushing the images from my mind until I can think of them more. "A quint in a physical union—like holding hands, you mean?" It sounds simple enough. "Should we try it, then, the five of us? Test whether the magic still works with a human?"

"No," Shade and Tye say together.

Shade spins me toward him. With his flashing wolf eyes and flexing jaw, it turns out the large male can be bloody intimidating. I lean away instinctively, but Shade's grip on my shoulders tightens. Not hard enough to hurt, but not gentle either. "No, Leralynn." Shade's low velvet voice is brutal. Unyielding. "Quint magic has killed fae before. You are mortal. Understand?"

My chest tightens, my heart beating hard and fast beneath Shade's relentless stare. The beautiful, hard planes of his face, framed by black hair mussed from the bed we just shared, are arranged in a shape I don't recognize. I pull against his grip again, meeting similar resistance.

"You made your point, Shade," Tye says behind me. Not a challenge, but a request. A plea on my behalf made from subordinate to superior. *So that's how it is.* River might be the commander, but the quint's hierarchy—whatever it is exactly—goes deeper, the subtle rank now plain in Shade's rigid posture and Tye's bent, supplicating face. Tye clears his throat. "She was just asking a question."

"And I want to hear her acknowledge the answer," Shade snaps at Tye. "Leralynn, you do not play with quint magic. You do not experiment. You do not connect hands with the four of us, no matter what happens. Do you understand me?"

My jaw tightens, this new side of Shade sending a shiver through me. "Yes," I hiss between ground teeth. "Let the hell go of me."

He nods his acceptance and tries to give my shoulder a gentle squeeze before releasing me, but I jerk free and stalk to the other side of the room. My hand closes around a hairbrush and Shade bows slightly as I sink the brush's teeth into my tangled hair.

"I'll show myself out," he says quietly, and I say nothing to stop him.

23

RIVER

*J*ust because River wasn't surprised at Klarissa's arrival didn't mean he was happy about it. As Autumn had warned him the previous night, the elder was indeed in Slait Court and had finally arrived at the palace a half hour ago, chasing away River's appetite for breakfast.

Now, River slipped his hands casually into his pockets and carefully avoided letting his gaze linger on Leralynn's perfect curves as he led his quint into the receiving room. The mortal wore a new outfit of Autumn's design this morning—loose silk pants the color of a fiery sunset, the cloth cupping her backside and swishing around her legs, and a tight white top that revealed a delicious swath of smooth skin at her midriff and crisscrossed over her otherwise bare back. Her auburn hair cascaded over her right shoulder, the loose strands on the left gathered into a teasing braid.

Autumn seemed determined to turn Leralynn into more and more of a fae female every hour the mortal spent here.

The last thing River needed. He was already sorely aware of her presence, her soft lilac scent that—

—that bloody clung to Shade and Tye as thickly as if they'd bathed in it.

River's spine stiffened. He wasn't jealous. He was beyond such pettiness when it came to his quint brothers. Plus, he couldn't permit himself such things as jealousy, not when keeping a clear head was his duty. To his quint, to his court, to the Citadel.

Leralynn had said she claimed them all, him included. Except there was a difference between being claimed and being wanted. River couldn't fault the girl, though, not when he could offer neither Tye's charm nor Shade's touch, which the male's wolf excelled at. After years of being his father's son, River's own soft places were protected behind a much higher wall than that. Even Coal, whose notion of a good training day could reduce any warrior to begging for mercy, could offer more to the girl than River could.

In that way, River and Coal were each other's opposites. The physical brutality that Coal could inflict and bear made River's stomach clench, yet when it came to a different kind of compassion, it was Coal who knew how to listen. Coal was River's third, but it was him, not Shade, whom River sought for counsel when his thoughts chafed too harshly.

Focus. River reined in his attention to the matter at hand. Klarissa and her companion had been shown to the receiving room a half hour earlier, and River couldn't make the elder wait much longer. River would have held this meeting in the bloody throne room if he didn't think his father would read the gesture as a personal assault on his power, but perhaps that would be too blunt a move anyway. As it was, the receiving room—set up like a library to create the illusion of intimacy—

was a strong choice to remind Klarissa that she was in Slait. It was a space that was entirely River's, from the plush leather armchairs to the two sofas and the choice of books lining the shelves. And of course, River's scent, which clung to every board and crack.

The servants had already set a pitcher of spiced wine on a low table—anything to wash away the taste Klarissa was sure to leave in everyone's mouth—and brought out delicious little pastries arranged on towering plates. River had requested the latter in hopes of tempting Leralynn. The girl hadn't had enough small pleasures like sweets in her life, and it was at least something he could offer. River liked watching Leralynn eat.

The council elder in question rose as River entered, her olive skin and gorgeously lined eyes as perfect as always. Klarissa wore a long forest-green gown today, leaving her shoulders open to the air, while her hair, an inky black, fell in a cascade of thick curls. If River were naive, he'd have thought the female had dressed up for him. But he knew better. Klarissa always looked stunning. Especially when she had murder and manipulation on her mind.

The male beside Klarissa, Pyker, River did not know well. Pyker was a Citadel warrior—and dressed like one, in fighting leathers and sturdy, practical clothing. His black hair was tied back at the nape of his neck to show off golden skin and dark eyes. Brown like Leralynn's, but not as rich. Not that any eyes could be.

It took all of River's self-control to seat himself away from the mortal girl, noting with approval that Coal and Tye had tucked her between them as they guided her to the couch. Coal, not Shade. That was surprising.

"Klarissa," River said with a nod that would be hard-pressed to call itself a bow. He might bow to her and the other elders at the Citadel, but here in his own receiving room, he would do no such thing. "Allow me to welcome you to Slait Court. Is there something with which I might be of assistance?"

Out of the corner of his eye, River saw Leralynn flinch at his ice-cold tone. Another crater between them that would have to be mended. But not now. Now, the flinching was good. As was the hard—almost cruel—set of River's jaw. The less Klarissa knew about River's true feelings, the better.

Klarissa's answering smile was frostier still. "I've come as a council elder to meet the commander of one of my quints, River, not the prince," she said, settling herself back on the couch and arranging the folds of her dress over her elegantly crossed thighs.

"You do me too great an honor," River replied dryly. "We would have attended the *whole* council at the Citadel shortly." He paused for a moment, letting that sink in. Klarissa was one of five on the council, and the others could sometimes keep her in check. "But as you are here, Klarissa, perhaps you could relieve me of the passage key and save me a trip."

Klarissa clicked her tongue. "Always so rash to jump to conclusions, River. Alas, youths often are. I am here to help you." The female's eyes shifted to Leralynn, sending a shiver down River's spine. "I understand that you have a small problem. A quirk of magic that chose a mortal where a fae warrior was needed. A regrettable situation that would permanently weaken your quint and put this poor girl in danger."

Tye's leg shifted, pressing into Leralynn's thigh. River held himself in check.

Klarissa frowned at her nails. "If my information is

correct, you were, in fact, on your way to the Citadel to request that the bond be severed. A most unusual request, but this is an unusual time, is it not?"

River kept silent. It was enough that Klarissa's spies had already informed her of the basics—River didn't want the female suspecting how little he wished to go through with the plan, or the size of the abyss that Leralynn's absence would leave in his soul. Stars, he wished he could keep Klarissa from so much as looking at Leralynn, much less speaking about her.

"Smile, River. I've come with good news." Klarissa's red lips parted into a smile of their own. "The council understands the difficult situation you are in and the urgent nature of your request. As such, we have already met and granted our approval."

River nodded stiffly, unwilling to let Klarissa see his reflexive fear. River had seen quint tethers cut in the past, when one of the five was so far in death's grip that hope was gone; it became better to give the remaining quint brothers a clean amputation. A clean cut also made it possible to attach another warrior to the injured quint, to let the bond heal with the new fae individual attached. The artificial bond never healed quite right, not the way natural magic connected the warriors—but it was better than the alternative black hole that might or might not ever be filled otherwise.

The window of opportunity for the procedure was so small that it was rarely possible—save when the death occurred on the Citadel training grounds, where the council had both the severing knife and a stable of waiting warriors available to find a fitting match.

River always thought it was too convenient a setup. Would as many quint initiates die during trials if the council weren't waiting to have one of their favorites bonded? The Elders

Council argued, of course, that the knife and waiting warriors were just a safety measure, that the training deaths were necessary to weed out the weak links that might lead a quint to a fate worse than death: capture by Mors forces.

So was it a coincidence, then, that Klarissa's trials had the highest death rate? That the warriors she chose to artificially attach to the desperate quints were once so very loyal to her?

The Citadel was vital in protecting against Mors's attacks, but that didn't make elders free from personal agendas and power plays. The other four council fae were mostly decent beings, but they all had a blind spot large enough to pull a cart through where Klarissa was concerned. If she was abusing the trials, they let her do it.

"Moreover," Klarissa continued, her voice light as a spring breeze, "there is no need to wait and fret. I am vested with the knife to part the tether here and now."

Now. The word sent an ice-cold shock down River's spine. Now was too soon. They were due to have a whole week more together, the time it would take to journey to the Citadel. A week more to savor Leralynn's company, to prepare themselves. A week wasn't enough—forever would not be enough—but River sure as hell wasn't going to deny the quint what little time they had.

"River." Klarissa's voice rang out in the silence that had stretched for far too long. "I am waiting for words of gratitude."

River's heart stuttered, the frozen shock melting to molten terror. He couldn't do it. Couldn't let Klarissa be the one to make the cut now.

Not now, not ever, River's soul whispered to him. *Your quint is full. Filled with the most precious gift possible.*

River rose, draining his yet-untouched wine goblet. "I have

long insisted that Citadel business and Slait business be conducted separately, Klarissa. I am not about to waver on that now. I will bring my case before you and the council at the Citadel, not here. Shall I have one of the servants show you out, or do you know the way?"

Klarissa's face darkened. Before she could speak, however, the male beside her, Pyker, bowed low in a silent request to be heard. "The council is aware that the severing procedure would leave your quint incomplete, Prince River," Pyker said, his tone strong but deferential. "As you've likely surmised from my presence, the elders believe it would be possible for me to heal into the bond. It . . . it would be the greatest honor of my life to serve beside you, Your Highness. And should you wish to test my skills before considering such a pairing, I am at your full disposal and command."

"Noted," River said, careful to keep his face still. Pyker sounded like he was truly requesting consideration, which went contrary to the council's usual method of providing a compatible fae warrior of their choice when the situation called for it.

River gestured toward the door and the others filed out obediently, Pyker bowing low again before departing. But Klarissa, the last besides River in the receiving room, stopped short. Twisting smoothly before the door, the female closed it behind her, trapping them inside together, and extended her finger to touch River's face.

River stepped out of reach, his jaw tightening.

"You can't mourn Daz forever, River," she said. "It isn't healthy for you. Especially since she is alive and happy with a family of her own now. The quint magic chose you, and she chose not to compete with that. Not everyone has the same outlook, you know."

"I am not taking you to bed, Klarissa," River said curtly. "Was there something else you wished to discuss?"

The female crossed her slender arms. "Your mortal," she said flatly. "The council is concerned that you are exposing the girl to undue stress and danger." She stepped close to River again, her nail tapping his chest. "Leralynn will be provided with everything she needs upon her return to the mortal realm. Money, clothing, shelter. Lunos magic ripped her away from her world, and the council will repair the damage." Klarissa paused, her voice dropping. "Stop using the riches of your palace to make Leralynn fear returning to her life, River. If you care for the mortal—and I've a feeling you might, your cold smile notwithstanding—you will ensure she is safe in a way she never can be in Lunos."

24

LERALYNN

*T*he meeting leaves me cold. Colder than Shade's stern side left me. Freezing.

In one swift moment I almost lost the quint, and despite knowing that moment was coming, it nearly shredded me apart. For every fiber in me that's grateful for the temporary reprieve, there is another cringing from the dark cloud of what's to come.

A bath. I want a bath and then I want Autumn.

"Leralynn." Klarissa's melodic voice catches me halfway down the corridor.

I turn toward the sound of my name, but somehow find Coal already there, pushing me behind him.

Klarissa opens her hands to show Coal her empty palms, then looks past the warrior to lock gazes with me. "Might we speak for a moment, Leralynn?" Klarissa asks, her voice silky with reason. "I promise to ask nothing of you, only to offer you information and answer any questions you might wish to ask. As one of the council elders, it is my duty to ensure your wellbeing."

I dissect Klarissa's words, looking for a trap. "How do I know you won't drag me into the Gloom?" I ask.

I expect the female to laugh at me, but Klarissa nods respectfully. "That is an excellent concern. I'm pleased that the basics have been explained to you. I do believe you would feel safer if Coal answered your query on my behalf. Coal?"

Coal crosses his arms, his eyes hard on Klarissa as he answers me. "She can't pull you into the Gloom because the palace is warded."

"Thank you, Coal," Klarissa says, as if praising a pupil. "Does that make you feel better, Leralynn?"

No. But I can't explain why either. Raising my chin, I step toward Klarissa, my shoes leaving indents on the soft rug. If she has information to offer, I'll listen. I can make up my own mind after that. Behind me, Coal growls softly but moves to the end of the hall, respecting my choice. "I'm listening," I say, my clipped tone adding a silent *for now*, which Klarissa ignores.

"I understand the past few days have been quite eventful for you," the elder says smoothly. She runs her fingers over the priceless fresco on the wall, as if studying the hounds painted there. "I'd say I know how you feel, but that would be a lie. To be frank, I've no notion of how quint magic affects a mortal. Though I understand that the differences are profound."

I keep my voice even. "Why do you say that?"

She shrugs one bare shoulder. "Because the quint went all the way to you. You did not go to them." She taps the wall, her nail drumming a rhythmic *click click click* against the plaster. "When the magic calls an immortal into a quint, the pull is too strong to be denied. Some die on their way. Coal clawed his way from Mors. But you . . . you didn't so much as leave your stable, did you?"

No. I didn't. I want to mull over what that means, but this isn't the time for it. I feel Klarissa watching, checking whether Coal's background shocks me, whether her insight into my own movements unsettles me at all. I offer her a simpering smile. "Ah. I see."

She smiles back, showing me her canines. "Did the males share with you how Kai died?"

No, again. I slip my hands into the pockets of my billowy silk pants, giving my hands something to do.

Klarissa steps away from the fresco and looks out the window, as if she can see beyond the manicured gardens of the Slait palace. She starts the story without waiting for my permission, and I'm helpless to stop her. "The quint had just dispatched a school of piranhas—small-minded worm-shaped creatures with five-foot-long bodies and a voracious appetite. The creatures usually stay deep in the Gloom but have been surfacing to feed more and more often the past hundred years. The fight was over, the quint victorious and resting. Shade, however, thought they might have missed something. Not wanting to disturb the others on a hunch, he stepped into the Gloom alone."

"You mean Kai," I correct.

"No. Shade." She frowns, her gaze still on the distant land. "Turned out that Shade was right. The quint *had* missed something—a gateway through which the slimy bastards had gotten into the Gloom shallows to begin with. While the quint was resting in the Light above, the piranhas were refilling the Gloom. And when Shade stepped back in, the whole school of them were on him in an instant. Sinking their needle-sharp teeth into Shade's flesh. Chomping off pieces."

Bile rises up my throat and I try to swallow without drawing attention.

"They'd gotten a jump on Shade, you see, and he couldn't return. But Kai was Shade's twin, and he felt his brother's life fading. So Kai rushed in after Shade and pulled him out. But . . . there wasn't enough of Kai left to save after that."

Blood drains from my head, making me dizzy. The images from Klarissa's story swarm in my mind. Stars.

"Shade couldn't defend himself," Klarissa continues, "and it took Kai's life to save him. That often happens in quints: It isn't the one in peril who dies, but the ones who go to his—or her—rescue." Klarissa's dark eyes swing to me, giving me time to absorb her words, to imagine who in the quint now could likely be in peril and who would be going to her rescue. Klarissa's voice drops so low, I can barely make out the words. "Listen to me, girl. The magic in those males' veins makes it physically difficult for them to separate from you, no matter how badly they wish to. It is easier on your end. If you've come to care for any of them, protect their lives by returning home."

My chest tightens and I nod, not trusting my voice.

"One other thing," Klarissa says, slipping a small red jewel into my palm. "If you need me, smear a drop of blood onto the jewel and I'll come to help."

LERALYNN

I stay where I am as Klarissa glides away, her feet silent on the plush carpet. Shifting a step over, I look at the fresco she was studying while we talked. A tranquil scene of a field with five identical hounds chasing an elusive fox through the brush. The paint is old, much of the plaster cracked with age, but beautiful nonetheless. The female covets beautiful things, I think.

Like River.

I flinch at my own thought. The reflexive jealousy it sparks.

"What was that about?" Autumn asks, stepping up beside me. Coal, still standing at the end of the corridor, leans against the wall, his arms crossed. Autumn slips her arm through mine. "What did that viper say to you?"

She showed me how dangerous I am. I swallow. "Klarissa told me about piranhas. How they killed Kai."

Autumn squeezes my hand. "There are much worse things than piranhas in the Gloom and Light both. The worms are vile, flesh-eating, swarming things, but mindless for the most part. It's the qoru I worry about, the sentient Mors dwellers. Them, and the Night Guard—the fae who've pledged allegiance to the Mors emperor."

"Why would anyone pledge allegiance to Mors?" I ask.

Autumn shrugs. "They are laying a wager that Mors will return to power, and when it does, they wish to be on the winning team. Point is that there is always something trying to kill us, so we might as well *live* now." She cuts a sly glance my way. "And those four weren't truly alive until you came."

The female turns her attention to the fresco and chuckles. "Oh, stars, you found this one, didn't you?"

I shake my head in confusion. "Is something amiss?"

There is a snort behind me and I turn to find Tye's amused eyes. "Oh, this one is good. Used to be even better."

Autumn points to the wall with her chin. "When River and I were a hundred or so, our mother insisted we study art. The master painted this one hound, and we were supposed to copy him over, twice each. Can you guess which ones are River's?"

I squint, looking closely at the identical pups. No, not identical. Now that I'm paying attention, I find one amazingly painted dog, two painfully careful imitations, and two . . . "Do these dogs have five legs?" I ask, afraid of touching the priceless wall, though no one else seems to be. "Wait, those aren't legs, they're . . . erm . . ."

"That's a young fae colt's idea of manhood," Autumn confirms.

"Oh, stars." My hand comes up to cover my mouth.

Autumn grins. "You should have heard the beating he got for that. He knew he would too. And you know what the stupidest part of the whole affair was? He could have told our mother he hated painting before it all started." Autumn pulls me along down the corridor, letting the silence settle for a moment before speaking again. "River isn't always good with reaching for words. Not when it comes to people who matter."

"Where are we going?" I ask, the longed-for bath quickly dissolving from plan to dream.

"Provisioning," says Autumn.

"What does that entail and why am I doing it?" I jerk my head toward Coal. "That one has the look of one planning a training session. It seems a shame to deprive him of the opportunity to bring me to tears."

"That one is coming with us." Autumn raises her voice, though I know fae hearing well enough by now to guess that the change is a simple formality. "You lot are setting out for the Citadel tomorrow and need, well, everything. River is dealing with the horses and I'm outfitting you and Coal. Tye has already stolen everything he needs."

The red-haired male blinks innocently. "I'm efficient."

I rub my face, the storm of Autumn's plans battling with the vestiges of Klarissa's words. *It isn't the one in peril who dies, but the ones who go to his—or her—rescue.* I let out a long breath, pushing the fact away for later. "So what's his job in all this?" I ask, pointing at Tye.

"The usual, I think—to be a pain in our ass," Autumn answers thoughtfully. "At least, that's the only job I've ever seen him do with any amount of skill."

"Oh, I have skills," Tye purrs in a way that makes my skin blaze hot with memory. "I'm along to offer my valuable opinion of Lilac Girl's clothing choices. And I think we should start the search by trying on undergarments."

I turn to Autumn, my eyes pleading. "He isn't really coming with us, is he?"

"He is," Autumn says grimly. "So is that one over there, who is feigning deafness."

That one over there—Coal—edges his way toward the door. "I have everything I need."

"You can argue with River all you want about that," Autumn informs him. "I'm certainly not going to. Now quit your whining and come along. Tye says he's interested in underclothes."

"Not *his* underclothes," Tye protests as the slender female sweeps all three of us up in her wake with the efficiency of a small hurricane.

I'M ALONE in my bed that night, having last seen Shade gnawing on a soup bone in the corner of the dining room. The wolf's eyes met mine for a moment just as he was opening his maw to engage his back molars against the crunchy cartilage, as if shouting *mine*.

I'm still unsure how to reconcile the furry wolf with the commanding warrior of this morning. One thing is certain: I've underestimated the power of these four from the beginning, having thought of only Coal and River as the truly dangerous ones. The power of Shade's voice—the confident, unyielding demand of it—is still echoing through my bones as I snuggle down into the covers, wondering how I can hate and want him so badly all at the same time.

I wake before the sun, pulling on new leather-lined pants that Autumn insisted River wanted me to have. All part of a kit that we assembled yesterday in preparation for the week-long journey to the Citadel. Having spent all the life I can remember at Zake's stable, the past few days of moving from place to place are feeding my nerves with a steady diet of anxiety and excitement that result in little sleep.

Slipping out of my room into the dark corridor, I go to step onto the plush carpet—only to trip over a large log that sure as hell wasn't there when I went to bed. The floor rushes up to meet me, my nose smacking into the rug. My hands go to my mouth to cover a yelp just as the damn log groans and opens a pair of offended yellow eyes.

"Argh." I collect my feet under me and rise as the log shifts into Shade's fae form.

"Why are you up this early?" he asks, sitting up and rubbing his eyes. He is once more without a shirt, and the carpet's pattern has made imprints on his skin. My hands long to run over the fatigued muscles, and I stick my hands into my armpits to keep the idea in check.

"Why are you sleeping outside my door?" I ask instead of answering him, looking down to assure myself that I am in fact dressed. Supple leather tucked into good boots and a close-spun red top wink back at me reassuringly.

Shade stretches, the six perfect squares of his abdomen shifting like velvet. "I didn't think I'd be welcome inside," he says quietly.

My cheeks heat, though a tingle low in my belly questions Shade's assumption. I sigh. "Why are you not in your own bed?"

Shade scratches behind his ear. With his hand, not his foot, at least. "I don't like leaving you unprotected," he confesses. "None of us do."

"Well, you can't be sleeping on the floor outside my door either," I point out in what I think are reasonable tones, which Shade promptly snorts at. I push the issue aside—there might not be any more bedrooms with doors between now and when

159

we arrive at the Citadel anyway. "Where is Coal sleeping?" I ask.

"He *was* sleeping in here," Coal answers from a door two paces away. Shirtless and wearing a pair of well-worn breeches, Coal ties his hair back as he steps into the corridor. "Why the bloody hell is the mortal up at this hour?" he demands of Shade.

I smile sweetly at him. "Because the mortal is going riding. And she thought you might wish to join her."

Coal's brow twitches. "The mortal doesn't know how to ride."

"Then the mortal is going falling," I say with a shrug, turning toward the stairs. "I'll give Czar your regards."

"Wait!" There is a small crashing sound as Coal grabs his boots, which he pulls on as he scrambles after me. "Czar is mine. Fall from your own bloody horse."

I stop, blinking at Coal as I process what he said. He smirks at me and pushes past, bellowing for River as he walks. The prince steps out from the room beside Coal's, looking exactly as he did when I saw him yesterday evening, in simple but finely tailored black pants and a white shirt.

"Did you sleep at all?" I ask the prince.

"No." He turns to Coal. "You shouted?"

Coal gestures lazily to my riding leathers. "Should we show her?"

River nods, a small, uncharacteristic smile touching his face.

My heart hops in my chest, my eyes narrowing at the males. Any upper hand I had this morning has clearly been usurped. "Talk."

"Leave Shade and come along, Leralynn," River orders, leading me and Coal through the dawn's breaking rays into the stable, where the familiar scents of leather, hay, and horse greet me with a friend's caress.

A curious mare sticks her nose out of her stall, whinnying sleepily at us. Coal stays behind with me while River walks farther in without lighting a lantern. Fae eyes. Fae sense of smell. Fae hearing. These beings are such predators that it's a wonder the horses haven't rebelled against them altogether.

After a few heartbeats, I hear the scrape of a bolt, the soft whisper of hinges, and the *clank clank clank* of a horse's hooves against the floorboards. Coal grips my upper arms, nudging me outside just as River leads out a gray mare I've not seen before. Small and muscular, with a gloriously thick silver mane and a star on her forehead, the horse is perfectly sized for me. The mare's large brown eyes study me intelligently.

My mouth dries.

"Mortal, meet Sprite," Coal says, stifling a yawn. "She was bred for her smooth gait, so even you should be able to stay on her."

My breath hitches, my eyes unable to shift from the mare. *Your own bloody horse.* That is what Coal said. I've never owned a warm cloak before meeting the quint, much less a horse. Stars. I swallow. "Is she truly . . ."

"Yours, yes," River says firmly. "The tack too. Don't let Sprite's small size fool you—she has a dexterity and endurance that any of the larger horses would envy. I think you'll enjoy riding her."

I am still catching my breath when I charge at River, deciding he deserves the first embrace. His eyes widen in surprise at the assault, but he catches me in a tight hold regardless, lifting my feet off the ground. Legs dangling, I press my cheek against his, feeling the cautious answering nuzzle that sends tingles of pleasure through my body. River smells of woods and soap, his powerful arms and the faint stubble against my face making me feel like I'm floating in a pool of danger.

I'm just deciding I might stay here forever when his next words pierce my heart. "She is yours forever, Leralynn," the prince of Slait whispers in my ear. "You can take her home when you go. You can take everything home."

26

TYE

"You were looking for me, Sparkle?" Tye said, leaning against the doorframe of the Slait palace library. The others were already outside, getting ready to leave now that breakfast was over. River had decided that, despite the relative safety of the Gloom in Slait, they would travel with Lera the old-fashioned way—riding through the Light. Tye couldn't say the decision upset him any, since he was in no hurry to actually reach their destination.

Autumn looked up from her table, barely visible to Tye behind piles of books and journals. As with her room, the objects entering Autumn's presence somehow immediately arranged themselves in the most disordered way possible. "No, but I was just about to," she said. "How did you know?"

Tye grinned. "What female wouldn't be looking for me the day I'm leaving?"

River's younger sister extended her hand, sending fiery sparks dancing and burning along Tye's ears. "You are insufferable."

Tye stifled the sparks, his grin growing. "Should I leave, then?" He knew the answer, of course. The only reason Autumn would be absent from the courtyard was that her brilliant mind was occupied with something else. Tye just hoped those thoughts were not spurred by the bastard calling himself her and River's father.

"Stay." Autumn waved him in, waiting for Tye to close the door, pull out a chair, and straddle it backwards. Her voice lowered. "I do need to talk to you. About Lera."

Tye's chest tightened, his body involuntarily tensing around his soul. He grinned lightly at Autumn, as she and everyone else expected him to, but he was dead tired of people talking about Lera. Discussing her necessary departure. Questioning her existence. It would take an effort of will not to snap the neck of the next person who called Tye's Lilac Girl a mistake.

"What if Lera isn't a mistake?" Autumn closed the book she was reading, a drawing of a four-corded knot betraying its contents as quint lore. Autumn crossed her arms. "Since when does magic make mistakes? Don't answer—I'm not convinced you can read, much less opine on matters of magical history. Point is, what if River is wrong?"

"If you are looking to convince someone that Lera is smart, beautiful, a little too brave, and frighteningly fitting for every wretched soul in our quint, then I'm already aware." *Too bloody aware.* "Want me to fetch River so you can say as much to him?"

"River will want facts," Autumn said frankly. "And I have no facts. I'm telling you because you think outside the rules."

"Rules are . . . like fences," Tye conceded. "They keep things nice and orderly, but he who hops over them gets the apples." And the thrashings. But that was beside the point. Autumn knew exactly who she was talking to. The female had been there during the quint's initial training, and she knew more of Tye than his own parents did. Which was probably a good thing for his mother's sleeping habits. "What's on your mind, Sparkle?"

Autumn hung her head with a sigh. "I don't know exactly. When you came back with Lera, you were all different. In a good way. As if your souls had found a missing piece of something. But I wonder if there isn't more to it. Bar the Elders Council—the only other mixed-gender quint ever to exist—you're the most powerful quint to have come out of the Citadel. Both in the strength of your individual powers and in the combined magic. How does your fire feel now?"

"Stronger still," Tye said carefully. "I've not tested it fully, but stronger than when Kai was alive."

Autumn nodded. "And Shade shifted form in the mortal lands. Do you know how impossible that should have been? Again, don't bother answering."

Tye blew out a long breath. "I'm the last person in Lunos qualified to discuss this, but even I must concede that while our individual powers are strengthened, our combined power is nonexistent. The quint magic has killed fae; it would rip Lera apart in a moment."

"Yes, yes," Autumn waved her hand. "I think you're right on that. I wonder if the magic strengthened your individual powers as compensation for Lera having none of her own. But there is something else too. Look at your quint now: a child of Slait, Blaze, Flurry, Mors, and now a child of the mortal lands. Doesn't that seem a bit too neat to be an accident? To be a mistake?"

"You are making my brain hurt, Autumn," Tye confessed, balancing his chair on its front legs. "I'm game for anything that keeps Lera with us. So tell me what you want me to do."

Autumn put her palms on the table. "Buy me more time to figure this out. Don't let the council cut the tether. Not yet."

Tye snorted and pushed off the chair, heading for the door. If he'd had any idea in hell as to how to stop the severing, he would have done it well before now. Autumn might need her books and calculations to figure it out, but Tye had known the truth in his heart and soul long since. It wasn't a matter of desire. It was a matter of ability.

In the courtyard, Pyker and the quint were already mounted, the playful breeze ruffling the fur of Lera's new cloak. Tye scowled. The garment did fit her perfectly well, but he much preferred seeing the lass wrapped in his own cloak. In his own scent. Lera was also, Tye noted, sitting atop her own horse. And doing it bloody well too, thanks to Coal's training.

"I don't like this," Tye said, glaring at Lera's high-backed saddle.

She bristled, checking her tack and posture, her voice low. "It took Coal two hours this morning to declare that I would more likely than not stay in the saddle without being tied to it. You are threatening to undo it all. So, pray tell me what *specifically* do you not like?"

"Everything." Tye's eyes narrowed accusingly at Coal. "It was my turn to have Lilac Girl ride with me. How is she supposed to throw herself into my arms if you've taught her to ride?"

"You'll figure something out, I'm certain," River said dryly, signaling the six of them into motion just as Autumn stepped into the courtyard, demanding that everyone in the quint— even Coal—return to embrace her goodbye.

Lera's gaze lingered on the small female as they finally rode out, a brave smile trying to conceal sad eyes. "I won't see her again, will I?" Lera asked.

"You never know," River replied, his eyes on the fields of wheat opening before them. The white-capped mountains beckoned from beyond.

The tightening of Lera's jaw said she'd heard the lie for what it was, just as Tye had. He kept his mouth shut, though, focusing on his horse's powerful movements—as if that could stave off the terror of all this becoming nothing but a distant dream where Tye had *her.* The fact that said *her* had the most exquisitely curved hips, a chest so ripe it begged to be suckled, and lips that made Tye's balls ache with need was bloody inconvenient.

Silently cursing Autumn, Tye nudged his horse to trot up to River's. "What if we don't do this?" Tye asked quietly, resorting to the truth for lack of other ideas. "I don't want the tether broken. I want her."

River's face snapped to him, the commander's gray eyes flashing violently. "You think you are the only one, Tye?" he demanded, baring his teeth.

Tye's blood heated in answering fury. "I'm not the one who is shoving Lera away with every other breath. One or two more pearls of wisdom from you and she'll think we're trying to get rid of her."

"We are on the way to the Citadel to sever her tether," River answered roughly. "What is she supposed to think?"

Tye's hands curled around his reins, the white-knuckle grip making the horse dance.

"Stand the hell down, Tye," River ordered.

The air around Tye heated. River did not take lightly to issuing such orders, and had this been any other topic, Tye would have backed down from his commander. But on this . . . on this he did not give an inch.

A deep growl rose from River's chest. "I feel as though a

piece of my soul has returned and the cut of that knife will sever it again," River said, the words hard, before his shoulders fell in a rare display of misery that drained the fire from Tye's own veins. "But tell me what the hell we have as an alternative? Connecting the five of us together will kill her. And even if we agree to never do that, what do we do then? Drag her defenseless into the Gloom? Leave her behind alone? Run off and become rogues, hunted by the Citadel and banned from the courts?" River shook his head. "I'll take any bloody option I can, but I have none."

"Then you are missing something," Tye said, falling back to watch Lera again. Autumn was right, she had to be. If they could just figure out what the magic intended before one cut of that knife destroyed them all . . .

Since Tye was already watching Lera's face, he was the first to notice her eyes widen, her mouth open with a scream that rang out just as he arrived at her side, his magic ready to burn the world. Around him, the other males were likewise reining in horses—even Pyker, who was at least smart enough to keep a polite distance from the rest of the group.

Lera pointed down to the ground directly under them, where a dark shadow the size of a small hut rippled beneath her horse's dancing feet. Living in the very earth. "The ground. There is something here."

Tye breathed out slowly, ordering his body to calm as he watched the darkness sprawl along the grass. "There is *something*, I'll give you that, lass. But the *here* part is not actually accurate. It's in the Gloom."

She swallowed and Tye wondered if he'd look too opportunistic if he offered to share his saddle with her now. As if reading his thoughts, River pushed his horse between Tye and Lera.

"Whatever it is, it won't come up here," River said.

"But it can come up somewhere?" asked Lera.

"Yes." River turned his face toward the mountain range breaking the line of the horizon. The neutral lands were close now, and while Tye would usually consider this a good thing, for once he shared his commander's concern. River raised his chin. "In the neutral lands, the wards are only as strong as the Citadel and quints can make them. Some parts are known for their thin barriers between the Gloom and Light, but depths and shallows shift as well. There are always breaches—sometimes natural, other times not. It's what keeps us employed."

Lera's face drained of color and Tye had the unreasonable urge to punch River in the nose. Unfortunately, that would be of little help in changing the truth.

"Here." Riding up to Lera, Coal withdrew one of his blades and held it out to her, hilt first.

Lera stared at the razor-sharp steel, her free hand dropping into her pocket to finger something Tye couldn't see. "I don't know how to use that," she said.

"The pointy end goes into your opponent," said Coal, his voice rumbling. "Take the weapon, mortal. I have more."

Tye snorted. "Yes, but do you know how to use the other one?" he called, grinning as the lass's bonny face turned bright pink while Coal's nostrils flared in delightful fury. Perhaps Tye might enjoy this ride after all—and he could work out the rest later.

27

LERALYNN

*W*e stop for the night at an outpost lodge at the edge of Slait Court. River dismounts first, coming over to help me down from Sprite's back. His hands grip my waist, lowering me slowly to the ground as his gray eyes drink in mine, emotions I'm having trouble reading racing through his gaze. I remember our embrace this morning, every inch of our bodies pressed together, how his wall came down for just a moment, and I wish we could get back there. Now he's the impenetrable leader again.

"Is everything all right?" I ask.

River nods quickly, stepping away. "The outpost isn't much," he says, gesturing to what looks like a hunting lodge that's worth more than what even the wealthiest of human nobles could afford. "But it's our last place to sleep with a real roof for a while."

"Who is going to cook?" Shade asks, already walking toward the forest. "I'll hunt."

No servants here, then. I'd volunteer but I've never had

enough food to learn to cook anything but the stew-of-everything. Coal catches my eyes and nods subtly, as if he's read my thoughts. Understood them without exchanging a single word.

"I'll cook," River calls over his shoulder.

"I'll take care of the horses," I offer tentatively, and I grin as Coal wordlessly drops Czar's reins into my hand.

"I'll take guard duty," says Tye. "What are we doing with the stray who invited himself along?"

Pyker flinches but raises his chin. He is a handsome male, with muscles as sculpted as the quint's, but I feel none of the tingling that the others evoke in me. What I do feel is the loneliness that comes from watching others talk and laugh and eat while you are kicked out to the stable. To the street.

A memory I've not seen in years burrows into my head. A flash of standing cold and lost and alone while families walked by, parents holding their kids tightly by the hand. No hand held mine, though. Not one. And I don't remember why.

"Klarissa's dog can sleep outside," says River, giving me his horse and walking to the lodge door. "There might be an empty stall in the stable too."

My spine straightens. "No." My voice rings loud enough to turn the males toward me. "No one is sleeping in the stable. Not to mention that Pyker may be a part of this quint once you are free of me, so maybe treat him with a straw of decency."

Silence reigns, five sets of eyes boring into me. The stable girl who thinks she can give orders to princes and immortal warriors. I brace for the coming cold shock of reality, raising my chin to meet it head on. I'll lose, of course, but I'll lose with dignity. Sometimes it is all one can do.

River shifts his weight, but it's Pyker who speaks first. "I'll be comfortable in the stable," he says quietly. "I enjoy the company of horses and can keep watch while I'm there."

"You will stay in the lodge, as Leralynn requests," River snaps, then twists back on his heels to continue inside. "Dinner should be ready in an hour."

WE START out early the following morning, the males quieter than they were yesterday. The weather is bright but chilly, leaves falling from the trees and fluttering in the wind. I'd expected the neutral lands to resemble the Gloom, but they look much as Slait did. Stunningly vivid and colorful trees, birdsong ringing from every cluster of branches, the breeze carrying the faint but constant aroma of wildflowers. After a swift run through a cluster of maple trees, their leaves dressed brightly for fall, we now trot along the base of a mountain range with a forest of evergreens spreading on our other flank, the occasional bit of river shimmering between the trees. Maybe the difference is visible in the Gloom, but I am not anxious to find that out.

The sun is just reaching its zenith when Pyker kicks his horse into a slow, controlled canter to come up beside River. "Sir," Pyker bows in his saddle, "I only bring this up because I rode this way recently, but it's too quiet."

"I like quiet," says Tye, grinning as he casually grabs my dropped reins and hands them back to me. His green eyes almost seem to glow under the high sun, and the crinkles around his smiling mouth make my chest squeeze.

River holds up a hand, stopping the group. "Quiet?" he asks Pyker.

The male nods cautiously. "It's likely nothing, sir. Just . . . It just feels different than it did a few days ago, when Klarissa and I passed through."

River sighs. "Something in the Gloom may have shifted. Coal, Shade, step over to the other side and check that we aren't about to have visitors. The barrier is feeling thinner here than I'd like."

The two males nod once and dismount, drawing their weapons and stepping into invisibility.

I shiver. "Shouldn't we go with them?" I ask, Klarissa's recounting of Kai's death all too clear in my mind. "Isn't your magic stronger if everyone is together?"

"Shade and Coal can handle themselves," River says, his back straight and his seat easy on the horse, but Pyker makes a sound in the back of his throat, his strained face betraying the truth of my words. They split up to keep me safely out of the Gloom, putting themselves in danger for it—exactly as Klarissa warned.

"River is right," says Tye, trotting forward to catch the loose horses. "Plus, I little want to step there today if I can help it."

I taste the words for the lie they are. Of course he wants to be with his quint brothers, fighting back to back instead of playing nursemaid to me. I reach into my pocket, where the stone Klarissa gave me burns my mind. The quint is taking care of me. Do I not owe them the same courtesy in return?

"Run!" River bellows, the cold, hard command making Sprite and me jump.

I grip my saddle, barely keeping my seat as I spin frantically to find what has the male on alert. I see it a heartbeat later, my mouth opening in a wordless scream as the air not ten paces behind me ripples and stretches to birth slithering brown worms. Slimy, ridged bodies thick as maple trees fall to the earth. Maws of needle-sharp teeth, absurdly white and large enough to gnaw off a leg in a single chomp, open and close blindly. Rhythmically. Hungrily. The soft, dragging sound of their movements makes bile rise up my gullet.

LERALYNN

*T*ye pulls up beside me, grabbing Sprite's reins again. "We need to run, Lilac Girl," he says, his voice icy calm. "Very fast. Hold on."

"No!" I jerk the reins from him, my hands shaking. My pulse races so hard that the world blurs, and Sprite dances beneath me as she senses my fear. "We aren't splitting up. You can't leave them. *I* can't leave them."

River is off his horse now, standing with his feet wide apart, his shoulders open to the piling beasts. And they are piling—five, a dozen, two dozen, too many to count. The breeze carries their rotten-egg stench to me and ruffles River's dark hair as the male holds his hand out toward the worms. An energy that makes my tongue tingle crackles in the air.

Then the very earth shifts. A crater two paces wide and twenty paces long opens between the worms and us, the creatures falling over its edge almost as quickly as new ones follow them from the Gloom.

Sprite's eyes roll in her head, the dancing and bucking

beneath me all too familiar. Thanks to bloody Coal, I know exactly when I'm about to get thrown.

"What the hell are you doing?" Tye demands as I slide from the saddle to the ground a moment before Sprite starts on her next bucking spree.

"Avoiding breaking my neck," I breathe.

Tye curses and swings down from his saddle, pushing me roughly behind his wide back while the horses run free and away, like the bright creatures they are. Ahead of us, the worms—*piranhas*, Klarissa's voice explains in my memory—continue to fill the crater, the vanguard building the foundation for others to fall upon.

"They will spill over shortly," River says. "I don't have enough energy to deepen the chasm." Calm. Matter of fact. As if a hundred man-eating worms fall out of the air every day.

Tye looks over his shoulder at me, his eyes drinking me in. "Your job is to stay alive," he says, the air around his hands swarming with lapping orange and yellow flames. "Don't get heroic. All right?"

"No danger of that," I say, my mouth dry. "Do what you need to do."

A short nod and Tye turns to step up beside River, his arms extended toward the crater. The smell of burnt rot hits me a few moments later as Tye's fire magic attacks the worms.

The creatures sizzle and steam but seem disinclined to catch fire.

"We'll have to do it the old-fashioned way," Tye calls, drawing his sword, his body moving with a dancer's grace as he splits the first escaped piranha in half. A second worm is already following, the never-ending pile of them refusing to slow.

I twist about, my own helplessness pounding me. Coal and Shade are still in the Gloom; River and Tye barely hold a school of piranhas at bay. The once-crisp air is thick with bile, rotten eggs, and the mute sizzling of the worms.

"If you want to help them, you need to stay alive," a voice says behind me. An arm in leather armor wraps around my waist, an unfamiliar bitter scent filling my nostrils. Pyker. The male bends his body protectively over mine as he turns to point toward the foothills a few hundred paces to our left. "There is a cave close by," Pyker says into my ear. "One with an entrance narrow enough that I can hold it myself. Can you run?"

I swallow. "The others—"

"The others need to be a full, real quint, not this perverted version of it," Pyker says bluntly, his arm pressing me into motion. "But they need to be worrying about protecting a bystander even less. If you can't be an asset, then at least stop being a liability. Unless you want to die and drain what power they have."

Pyker's cold words wash through me, the truth of them stinging my nerves. The cave. Yes. Close and protected so no one need worry for my sake.

"All right," I breathe, letting the male pull me along as I focus on my feet, willing them to move faster toward the cave. "Where is it exactly?"

Pyker points with his sword at something still a hundred paces off. Maybe more.

"We've different definitions of 'close by,'" I pant, my lungs burning.

"Move, human," Pyker yells, slowing to match my shorter strides. Behind us, the sounds of battle—cracking earth, the spit and crackle of flames, the thick, wet thuds of swords slicing worms—are deafening for their quiet rhythm. "Faster. Run for your life—and your quint's life too."

I do. I focus on the pounding of my feet, begging my muscles and lungs to work through the pain, willing myself to reach the cave mouth growing before us.

"Bloody stars." The change of tone in Pyker's curse jerks me from my survival trance.

I look up to see a dark-clad figure with a sword rushing at us from the very opening Pyker and I are headed for. The dark fae warrior's steel flashes in the bright sun, Pyker's own blade coming up to meet it with a deafening clash that has me screaming in spite of myself.

The new male pulls back, spinning with his next blow. The blade cuts so quickly that I hear the whistle of air along the steel as it swings for Pyker's side.

Pyker's blade snaps down and he grunts as he parries the blow. His other hand sweeps out to grab me, pulling me behind him. Protecting me with his body the way Tye did.

Except it isn't working the same way, because Pyker's body is moving too. Spinning. A slave to the recoil of his last parry. He's lost control, I realize with an icy shock. Pyker has lost control, and this wild attempt to save me will get me cut to pieces instead.

I shove away from him, summoning all my strength to throw myself clear of the melee.

Instead of releasing me, Pyker's arm tightens, and a second realization strikes me with cold clarity.

He never lost control.

A trap. This is all a trap to get the quint separated. To get me killed despite Pyker's heroic attempts to save my life. To pave the way for the males—*my* males—to welcome Pyker into their fold.

I am too angry to even scream as Pyker swings me directly into the path of the dark warrior's coming blade.

The male catches my gaze, grinning wickedly as he swings for my neck. A fountain of red blood splatters his brown tunic.

I wait for the pain. The dizziness. The darkness.

The world stubbornly refuses to so much as blink.

So I blink instead. Blink and realize that the blood on the dark male's clothing is his own, spurting around the tip of Coal's blade, which has just pierced the bastard from back to front.

Pyker steps away from us, his breath heavy, his eyes wide. "Thank the stars—" he starts to say.

"Down!" Coal orders, throwing himself on top of me, pinning me beneath his muscular frame.

My head rings from the impact against the ground. In the sliver of daylight between Coal's body and the earth, I see an arrow flying down at us from the cliffs. Then another. Another still. For a heartbeat, confusion rushes through me. At least one of the projectiles should have hit us by now. Surely the high-up archer isn't so bad as to miss a stationary target, shot after shot.

One heartbeat and then I realize the truth. The archer *is* hitting us. And Coal is taking each and every arrow as he continues to cover me in silence.

29

LERALYNN

The world around me slows. Each contraction of my heart lasting an eternity as reality lays itself bare before me. It is amazing how clear the truth is when stripped to the bare facts.

The archer will continue firing.

Coal is going to die.

Unless I buy Coal's life with my own.

My gaze shifts, finding Pyker standing before us, making a show of being a shield against an archer who isn't aiming for him. Still working on that illusion.

Good. That is the one piece of leverage I have on Pyker—Coal's ignorance of Pyker's treason and Pyker's desire to keep it that way.

"Pyker," I command from beneath Coal. "Pull me into the Gloom."

"No," Coal growls, the fury vibrating through his injured muscles, his precious breath warm in my ear. "Piranhas there."

Of course there are piranhas there. There must be, if they

are spilling out into the Light. But since I'm going to die anyway, facing a few worms seems to little matter. Ignoring Coal's protest, I lock eyes with Pyker. "Pull me into the Gloom," I tell him again. "It's safer for me there."

Pyker's eyes narrow. It's death for me there, and he knows it. But he also knows that I know of his treason. And he understands my request, if not my reason for making it. *Pull me into the Gloom, Pyker, and there won't be anyone to contradict your account when I die.*

Pyker's hand reaches for mine.

"No!" Coal gasps, his breath failing. "Not. Safe. For. Her."

"I want the Gloom," I say loudly, grasping Pyker's extended arm and smiling sadly as Coal's desperate roar to his quint brothers follows me out of the Light.

With the next breath, I am there. Here. The river, the path, the mountain—it's all as it was a moment earlier. Except not. The sparkling water is dull, the grass gone, the moss growing on the rock face thick and glowing with a faint blue tint. A washed-out, wrinkled version of the upper world.

"Satisfied?" Pyker says, letting go of my hand.

Ignoring him, I twist about, getting my bearings. Distances are different here—smaller, if I've wagered right based on Coal having gotten to me as quickly as he did.

Yes. The mass of piranhas that was a hundred paces off in the Light is less than twenty steps away now, the slithering mass crawling up, up, up into the nothingness that I know is their gateway into the Light. The cavern River opened doesn't exist here. Interesting.

"Where are all the piranhas coming from?" I ask Pyker. Not that it matters, but I'm curious.

The male points to the center of the crawling worms. "A deeper level of the Gloom. The wards are thin here, it seems."

Pyker's voice is dull. "They will smell you in a moment, though. You'll forgive me for not waiting around until—"

He breaks off as the air ripples and the four quint males step—or in Coal's case, crawl—into the Gloom. Coal is beside me already, the others rushing from where they fought piranhas moments ago. Except it's all closer now. We are all closer. The quint separated to protect me, but at least that problem is now corrected.

River's eyes flash with a fury I can see even in the Gloom. "Why the hell are you here, Leralynn?"

Because I knew you'd come for me. Now come closer still. We've more to do. My gaze shifts to Coal, my throat burning. Several of the arrows failed to make the trip with him and their empty wounds now bleed freely.

Shade kneels beside Coal, the healer's face grim.

"Shade, you have Coal," River shouts as he and Tye step toward me. "Tye and I will take Leralynn."

A noble attempt to save our lives, but even I know it won't be enough. Fortunately, I'm about to correct the lack-of-power problem. Careful not to bring attention to myself, I press my foot against Coal's arm as the other two close in.

River grabs my wrist.

I grab Tye's.

There. Five. Shade touching Coal. River gripping me. Me pressing my skin against Tye and Coal both.

River's eyes meet mine and widen just as the first wave of power pulses through our bond.

"I've claimed you, River," I say before he can pull away. Speaking is hard. Not because of pain, but because of a sudden awareness of everything at once. Every sound. Every smell. Every taste. Every touch. "The quint is mine, as I am yours."

My words falter with the next wave of power. And with it, there is no longer a Lera. No anyone else either. There is only the quint, our hearts beating as a single great force. I was planning to be dead. Instead, I'm more alive than I've ever been.

River hesitates only a moment before realizing what he must do. He lifts the hand not touching me and a wave of raw magic ripples before us. If I could choose where to look, I'd turn away from the writhing pile of piranhas splattering into a mass of goop. If I could move, I'd flinch away from the agony of magic searing Coal's wounds closed. If I could speak, I'd shout about Pyker fleeing back into the Light.

But as I can do none of these things, I just hold on to River and Tye and Coal and Shade, and I entrust my life essence to them forever. *They can have it all.* The last thought is oddly peaceful, and I smile as the world finally dissolves into darkness.

30

LERALYNN

I wake to the scent of citrus and pine and the rhythmic rustle of running water. The sun piercing my eyes blinds me for a moment, until something beneath me shifts, veering my face away from the inconsiderate rays. The cold air nips my face, but an insistent warmth seeps through my back and sides, balancing the chill. Which all leads to one undeniable conclusion. "Why the hell am I naked and in your lap, Tye?"

The green-eyed male grins down at me. "You must be in paradise."

"If I'm in paradise, then stop ruining it with your cold hands," I mumble, though it does no good, as Tye's fingers continue stroking my face and forehead. I try to sit up, but Tye's hold tightens and River's concerned face appears in my field of vision.

The quint commander crouches beside me, his liquid gray gaze piercing into my own. I want to reach up a hand to smooth the worry lines on his forehead, but the wall he keeps around him is firmly in place.

"How is Coal?" I ask.

"Yes, in case you were wondering, you are alive, Leralynn," River says flatly. "Not that you should be after your mortal body conducted enough magic to knock out a herd of horses, but you are."

"For the time being," Tye clarifies. "We make no promises once Shade learns you're awake."

"Is he very mad?" I ask.

"For tricking us into doing the one and only thing none of us were willing to risk?" Tye says, his hand still stroking my face. "For utterly disregarding the one demand he made of you? What do you think?"

"I think I might prefer piranhas' company." I shimmy to sit up more, relieved to see that Tye has at least covered me with a cloak. None of which explains why I'm naked to begin with. And as far as I can tell, so is Tye. "Did the magic kill my clothes, or is this your way of keeping me from running off from . . . Where are we exactly?"

"About a mile from where we were," says River, and I look around what appears to be a partially covered alcove in the side of the mountain. A natural rock wall separates the space into two chambers, the water I heard earlier running over the partition in a tiny waterfall and feeding an outgoing stream. Ahead of us, the evergreen forest and distant river wink in the sun. "And you lack clothes because you were freezing and skin-to-skin contact was the most efficient way of warming you."

I turn back to the rocks, blinking at the glowing blue moss covering them. No. I shake my head, clearing my vision. No blue moss. Just a bit of natural yellow and green growth.

"We've been trying to warm you for five hours," River tells me, tucking the cloak tighter around my shoulders. His gentle fingers and careful fussing are so at odds with the no-nonsense commander I've come to know that I feel a sudden lump of tears in my throat. Tye draws me closer still, my back pressing against his smooth, sculpted chest. "The Gloom consumed your heat. That, at least, is normal." River blows out a long breath. "Are you hungry?"

My stomach growls, answering River's question before I can even check in with my own body. Great.

"How is Coal?" I ask again, now pushing against Tye in earnest. My memories return in a vengeful storm. The arrows. The blood. The searing pain. The desperate need to do something, anything, to keep him alive. What if I failed? My heart stutters. Coal took arrows meant for me, and the last I remember seeing him, he was dying. "Where is he?" I'm shouting now. "Is he . . . is he—"

River catches my shoulders, looking into my eyes to ensure that his words penetrate. "Coal is alive. In more pain than he'll admit, but Shade was able to staunch the bleeding in time. Fae heal faster than humans. All right?"

I nod, not realizing I'm shaking until River leans forward, adding the heat and strength of his body to mine. His scent blends with Tye's, the two of them holding me in a tight cocoon of safety and warmth, and I cling to both males, unbidden tears rolling down my cheeks.

A too-short eternity passes before the sound of footsteps interrupts us, and River squeezes my shoulder before leaning away to look behind him. My gaze follows his, stopping dead at the familiar sight of Coal's muscled body.

I swallow, wiping my face quickly.

"Shade is hunting dinner and the horses are grazing," Coal tells River. He holds his body rigidly, nothing like the lithe panther I know him to be, but my gut warns me to feign blindness to Coal's soreness just as fiercely as Coal pretends not to see my tears.

"Pyker?" River asks. "Has he become any more talkative?"

Coal goes to cross his arms, winces slightly, and lets them drop to his sides. "The prisoner confessed to leaving bait for the piranhas and paying the two bastards to hide in the mountains and attack the mortal. All to convince us to let him join the quint."

"Klarissa." River's voice is ice.

Coal shrugs. "Of course. However, Pyker will not admit to it, and the one male who showed himself is long dead. But Klarissa did leave the severing knife in Pyker's care."

River snorts.

"Klarissa will say it was simple precaution given the nature of our quint," Coal continues, then pauses, letting the silence hang as his eyes finally find mine, a thousand emotions streaking through that purple-tinged glance. Relief. Fury. Need. Violence. Worry.

I press deeper into Tye's arms, wondering if I might be able to will my body into an instantaneous sleep.

"I'd like to speak with the mortal, please," Coal says. "Alone."

"I have a half hour open on my schedule early next week," I mutter.

River, coward that he is, rises smoothly and disappears behind the rock partition that splits this little makeshift shelter in two. Tye is slower to rise, ensuring that I'm wrapped up in the cloak before settling me on the ground. Tye, at least, is wearing his small clothes, though not much else.

My cheeks heat. *Five hours. I wonder whether they took turns warming me.*

"Like what you see?" Tye says, catching my gaze and stretching languidly.

"Not particularly," Coal answers dryly before I can conjure up a reply.

Tye turns to the other male and makes a derisive sound in the back of his throat. "That is because you are unable to appreciate the finer things in life, Coal. If you think it's only females who know a good thing when they see—"

"Get the hell out," Coal says.

Tye grins, contracts his pectorals in a muscle wink, and saunters away before Coal can assault him.

Left alone with Coal, I struggle to gather my legs under me and get up. It's already bad enough that I'm naked beneath the cloak; I don't want to additionally imitate a puddle.

"Don't bother," says Coal. "Even if you do manage to stand, I'm taller than you anyway."

"Good for you."

Shaking his head, Coal lowers himself to the ground, crouching before me. Weighing me with his gaze. The square cut of his jaw is tense, the clenching muscles stretching his taut skin. Coal's hair is pulled back into its usual bun and glistens as if washed recently. He wears a sleeveless black shirt, and his wrists, braced comfortably atop bent leather-clad knees, show those horrid scars. The foot of space between us vibrates as words race through my mind but refuse to form on my tongue. I want to lean into him, thank him, run away from him, kiss him. All at the same time.

"I was going to die," Coal says finally, his face so still that I can't read the emotions beneath.

191

"They were shooting at—" I start to say, but he shakes his head.

"I mean that I was prepared to die. It was a choice I'd made. A choice I had the full right to make."

I draw my knees up to my chest and tip my face up. "If that's what you really want, I'm sure it can be arranged."

Coal doesn't smile. He watches me, those brilliant blue eyes tinged with a bit of purple that is as hidden as it is mesmerizing. "It wasn't because I do not value my life, but because it would have been worth it. Because you are worth it, mortal."

A shiver runs through me. I'm more used to Coal trying to kill me than being kind, and this turn of events prickles uncomfortably. So I do what Coal would do. Ignore it. Talk about something else. Except the words that bubble from my chest aren't the ones I wanted. "I was going to die too. When the five of us joined, it was supposed to kill me. But . . . Maybe you are worth it too, you bloody bastard." An uninvited lump forms in my chest. Trust Coal to dig through until he finds whatever makes you tremble. "Can we not talk about it?"

"Were you scared?" Coal asks.

I growl softly and bite my lip. Thinking back to those moments is more difficult than it should be, given how everything turned out. But reality seems to have little respect for what it should and should not be like.

Coal waits.

"No," I say finally.

He cocks a brow.

"Yes?" I groan when he only blinks like a damn owl. "What do you want me to say?"

"Start with the truth and we'll go from there," Coal suggests.

I sigh. "At first, yes," I say. "When I realized that . . . that you were hit. Bleeding. I was very frightened then."

He nods but keeps his silence, as if knowing what I need to find my words. And he is right.

"Then, when I had the idea about connecting us, when I decided to tap into the power of five, the fear faded. I didn't *think* I was going to die; I *knew* I would, and I was all right with that so long as I forced the quint to connect." I draw a breath. "And then—I mean now, when I didn't die, I'm scared all over again. About what could have happened, what did happen, about everything."

For the first time since he came up beside me, Coal touches me, laying a hand on my cheek, his thumb sweeping a soft line along the bone under my eye. Warmth travels from that point and spreads through my body, warming me almost as well as Tye's chest did. For a moment he's silent, scanning my face as if making sure it's all still there. "Me too, mortal," he says quietly.

Relief eases my chest, tingling over my skin.

Coal drops his palm to my shoulder and gives it a squeeze, which in Coal's world is probably the equivalent of a bear hug. "Just so you know, I will train you to fight for however long you wish. A lifetime. There is no limit."

"A lifetime? But that's only possible if . . ." My eyes narrow, Coal's words finally penetrating. If I want to stay in Lunos, then Coal at least will have me. Mortal and all. Stars.

He rises quickly, before I can finish my thought.

"One other thing," Coal says, his voice returning to its usual briskness. "Shade will have a few things to say to you when he calms enough to speak. In short, I don't envy you, mortal, but you are on your own for that one."

"Coal building me up so I can face Shade?" I throw up my

193

hands. "Did the world turn on its ears while I was in the Gloom and forget to turn back?"

A small smile touches the corners of Coal's mouth. "Shade is a big, fuzzy *wolf*, mortal girl. Don't let his good table manners distract you from what he eats for dinner."

LERALYNN

The sun is setting behind distant trees when I finally see Shade. The male, in his wolf form, is returning from a hunt to drop off a pair of fat rabbits beside the fire River built. Shade's yellow eyes flash at me in the firelight as he turns away, lifts his tail into the air, and trots back to the forest.

I follow him toward the edge of camp, glad to finally be in my clothing—Autumn's finely tailored leather-fortified riding pants and a red tunic that tucks in at my waist, beneath a furry overcoat. Despite the warm coat I have on, straying far from the fire is difficult, the Gloom's chill still racing through me with each small blade of wind. "We've five rabbits and a deer already, Shade," I call to the wolf's retreating form. "I think that can hold us over for an hour or two."

The wolf hesitates, his body bending as he turns to look at me over his shoulder. Our gazes meet. One of Shade's ears twitches and then he turns away from me again, disappearing into the trees.

I sigh and return to the fire. Tye is already roasting a

sizzling piece of meat, the smell making me moan a bit with hunger. Sitting beside him, I content myself with pining after dinner and am just starting on my second rabbit leg when Shade appears again.

"Hello," I tell the wolf.

Shade adds a squirrel to our growing stockpile and turns away.

"The meat is going to go bad," I yell after him.

Tye snorts. "The meat will be gone by morning, Lilac Girl. Using magic will leave you starving."

"I don't know if what I did counts as using magic. I just conducted it through me."

"You really want to debate magic theory now?" says Tye.

"No." I sigh. Despite a still-growling stomach, my appetite disappeared with Shade. Wrapping my coat tightly around my shoulders, I walk to the edge of camp and find a spot to sit. Not so far as to be out of the males' sight, but far enough away to allow Shade to yell at me in private—whenever he finally gets around to it. There is little point in putting off the confrontation, since I know I won't be getting much sleep without his warm body pressed against mine.

I see the yellow eyes watching me a good quarter hour before the male himself appears, walking in his fae form out of the high brush. My breath hitches at the beautiful planes of his face, revealed by dark hair pulled back at the temples. At the chest muscles shifting beneath his loose linen shirt. At the storm raging in his golden eyes, a twin to the one that crackled there when we faced off in my palace bedroom. A simmering, rigid Shade.

Stalking silently to where I sit, Shade settles on the ground beside me, his face raised to the fat moon hanging overhead.

"You aren't going to bay at the moon, are you?" I ask

finally. A week ago, I didn't know the damn male existed, and now all I can think about is easing the tension between us.

"No," says Shade. "I don't feel the pull today."

I sigh, pinching the bridge of my nose. "For the sake of efficiency, let's just acknowledge that I did the one thing you demanded I never do—connect myself with the full quint. Let us also acknowledge that I am not the least bit sorry and I would do it again in a heartbeat. Now, with this out of the way, please feel free to yell or growl or do whatever you planned to as much as you wish."

Shade is silent for a moment, still watching the sky. "Efficiency," he repeats, tasting the word.

"Efficiency," I confirm with a nod.

He leans back on outstretched arms. "I'm immortal," he says flatly. "I'm not attracted to efficiency."

Silence settles between us again, which only makes waiting for the eventual storm that much harder. My limbs shift, the tension in my muscles making it impossible to stay still in the way Shade seems to have perfected. I bite my lip and a tick rattles a muscle in Shade's jaw, betraying how aware he is of each of my movements.

Aware and unyielding. The space between us is no more than two feet, yet it might as well be a piranha-filled crater for how likely Shade's hand is to breach it. I feel that lack of touch more keenly than I've ever felt a blow.

"Did you give Coal this hard a time as well?" I ask. "Because what he did, taking all those arrows, it wasn't much different. So I'm thinking it is only fair that he and I receive the same treatment."

Shade squints at the stars dressing the velvet sky. "Coal and I spoke, yes. I was extracting arrowheads from him at the time, however. It's fascinating just how tightly you can hold

197

someone's attention when you're about to dig a piece of barbed steel from the sensitive spot just under the shoulder blade here." He presses a finger into my back, hard enough to tease a slight flare of pain. A mere tiny fraction of what Coal felt.

I shudder. "Yes." I swallow, licking moisture back into my lips. "I imagine one's attention would be quite undivided in those circumstances. Even Coal's. Fortunately, no such measures will be necessary with me. Please scold away at your convenience."

Shade pushes off his arms, sitting up straight. And just like that, the calm veneer shatters to pieces. "You don't get to kill yourself," he snaps, the vibration of his voice more potent than I expected. "Whatever the problem, suicide is not the acceptable solution. No discussion. It isn't. If you were a wolf, I'd be grabbing you by the scruff of your neck right now and shaking you until your teeth rattle."

Despite expecting it, the sheer force of Shade's onslaught singes my nerves, the fear and fury in his voice burning my core.

"I'm sorry——"

"Sorry won't help if I lose you."

"No." My voice is even despite my pounding head. "It won't. That wasn't an apology for fighting, by the way; it was an expression of empathy for your worry."

That does it.

Shade growls at me. His eyes are feral, his words a barely leashed violence. "You don't get to get yourself killed. Never. Not for us, not for me."

My chest aches for him. I tilt my head back, looking up at the same sky Shade was studying moments ago. "Are we talking about me or Kai?" I ask finally.

Shade stills, the tension in his muscles rippling through the air. "What?"

"Klarissa told me what happened with your twin," I say quietly. "How you went into the Gloom alone. How Kai went after you. How only you returned."

Shade leans away.

I grab his wrist. "Don't you dare shift into a fuzzy puppy to avoid this conversation," I say, looking right into those large yellow eyes. "Or we'll see just who shakes whom by the scruff of the neck."

Shade growls again, showing his teeth, but it's different from before—defensive. He remains in his fae form. "It wasn't Klarissa's story to tell."

"No," my grip tightens. "It was Kai's story. He was the one who made the choice. You don't get to take that away from him, Shade, to say what his priorities should have been."

Shade's eyes flash, his shoulders rising with rapid breaths. He tries to jerk his hand back, but I'm ready and hold on with all my might. Instead of freeing himself from my hold, Shade's movement pulls me closer to him. The male's nostrils flare and he growls into my face.

I don't pull away. I don't even flinch. My knees settle beside Shade's thighs and I place my free hand against his sweaty cheek.

"It wasn't his choice to make," he says.

"Whose choice was it?" I ask softly.

"*I* went into the Gloom," Shade whispers. "I went. I made the choice. Me. No one else. I was cocky and confident and reckless and stupid. And—" He cuts off his words. A snarl that's meant to be vicious but is brimming with pain instead escapes his chest. "You know what happened next."

I rise high on my knees and bring my forehead to rest

against Shade's. Feel the trembling of those powerful muscles. My heart longs to wrap Shade in my arms, easing his thoughts. But I don't. Can't. I owe him better than that.

Ten years. He's spent ten years avoiding these memories. And it's time for Shade to return in soul as well as body.

I make my voice hard. A wolf, Coal reminded me, Shade is a wolf. And sometimes wolves need a nip. "Say it."

"I can't," Shade whispers.

My heart tears, but I don't let the male escape. Not from this. The heat of our bodies fills the air. "Say it, Shade. You made the choice. You went into the Gloom. And then?"

"And then a school of piranhas was there. And I could have left, but I didn't. I went after them for bloody bragging rights. I didn't see that they were coming from the Subgloom, that there wasn't an end to their masses. And then it was too late. There is a paralytic on their teeth, and one chomped down on me the wrong way. They were so slow, those damn worms. And I was fast. Until I couldn't move at all."

"And then?"

"And then I kept my mouth shut," Shade stutters, his voice rising with each new word. "But Kai was my bloody twin and he sensed my peril anyway. So he came. And then he died. It should have been me, but it was him. Is that what you wanted me to say, Lera? I am the one who should have died. Me."

I press my mouth over Shade's, pouring every ounce of understanding and compassion and resolve into the kiss. The large male freezes beneath my touch but his lips yield to mine, his heart pounding so hard I feel it through our touching chests.

"Kai wanted you to live," I whisper, pulling away from Shade's mouth to draw breath. "Stop sulking because you didn't get consulted, and get the hell out of that ten-year-old piranha pit. We need you here, Shade. I need you."

Shade stills, my last words hanging between us. My own body goes still as well, my heart stopping for a moment before sprinting into a neck-breaking gallop. I meant the words for Shade, but the truth of them recoils into my soul, ricocheting with merciless power. I do need him. I need them all. I love them.

Stars. I pull back from Shade, my eyes wide. *I don't get to love them, not without them dying for it.* Hell, I nearly got everyone killed just crossing a stretch of land, and if we stay together it will only get worse. I'm a distraction at best and a bloody target at worst. I study Shade's beautiful, strong face. The silver lining his yellow eyes. Kai loved Shade enough to ensure he lived. And though I've never met Shade's twin, I understand Kai completely.

I'll do whatever must be done to keep the males alive.

"Cub?" Shade asks, reaching his hand toward me.

I jerk back. Get to my feet. Dip my hand into my pocket to feel Klarissa's stone. I know what I must do, and that I need to do it quickly, while I'm still brave. There is only so much willpower inside me, and I'm down to the very last drop. Pulling out the stone, I bite my lip hard enough to raise a bead of blood.

"What's going on?" River's voice cuts through the air as he strides toward us, the other two behind him. I wonder whether they smelled the blood or just saw me jump to my feet.

"What the hell did you do, Shade?" Tye demands.

"I will kill you, wolf," Coal growls softly.

Shutting my eyes, I press the stone quickly to my bleeding lip, flinching at the sudden flash of magic that sparks and vanishes into thin air. My chest tightens and I drop to my knees, letting the bloody stone roll free from my palm as I drink in the males I love.

"What did you do, Leralynn," River whispers, picking up the stone. "What is this?"

I force myself to sit up straight, proud of my dry eyes and steady voice. "I've summoned Klarissa. I'm ready to go home now."

River's face darkens, his eyes wide. With a roar, he throws the stone against the mountain face, his shoulders vibrating as the jewel bounces. "Like hell you are going anywhere," he yells, turning back to me.

My jaw flexes. This is hard enough without the quint commander himself cracking. "You don't get to tell me where I'm going, River," I say shortly.

"Fine." River shows me his teeth as he steps closer to me. "But in that case, I'm going with you."

"Me too," says Tye.

"As am I," Shade whispers.

Coal crosses his arms, nodding silently along with the rest.

I throw back my head, waiting for the stars themselves to laugh at the males. Or at me. "Go with me to where, River?"

"The mortal lands, I presume," he answers.

I throw up my hands, twisting back to the males. "The mortal lands? What the bloody hell are the four of you going to do in the mortal lands?"

"Wear lots of hooded cloaks, I suppose," Tye says, fingering his pointed ears. "The humans are strangely disturbed by all the wrong things."

I shake my head at them, my heart pounding. "You are elite fae warriors of the Citadel," I say, slowly enough that even one soft of mind could comprehend. "You need to be alive to kill bad things coming from Mors. I am a human. I will get you killed. Hence, we are severing the bond and I am going back to the mortal lands while you four bastards stay here and try to do your job. End of discussion."

Tye scratches the back of his head. "See, there is one problem with that, lass. Even Klarissa can't force-cut the bond. Either someone must be very near dead or everyone must agree. You are of course welcome to spend the rest of your mortal life trying to convince us to agree—or trying to get yourself killed, I suppose. But short of that, it won't actually work."

"Why?" The question tumbles from my lips. "Why would you want me?"

Shade reaches forward as suddenly as the words are out, taking my face firmly between his warm palms. "Because we love you, cub," he says roughly. "And we can't do otherwise."

LERALYNN

a campfire's crackling flames. The rhythmic beat of the waterfall. Shade's strong arms wrapped around me protectively. My nose pressed into his warm chest. Perfect as it all is, none of it can quiet my heart's sudden gallop when Tye steps out of the Gloom and nods subtly.

Klarissa is almost here—approaching us in the Gloom. Two hours after I used my blood on her stone to call out to her. Even traveling through the Gloom, that she made it here in two hours means the female was close by already. Just waiting for my call.

I meet Tye's eyes, expecting him to say as much.

Instead, the red-haired male bristles and twists toward River. "Why is my Lilac Girl in that dog's lap?" He braces his hands on his hips. "Need I remind you that the last time we left the two of them alone, he nearly chased her away?"

River tears off a juicy rabbit quarter, shaking off the drops of fat. "What do you want me to do about it, Tye?"

Tye settles on the ground and pats his thigh. "Tell her to sit on my lap instead."

Shade licks his canines.

"Are you two serious?" I hiss just as Coal joins us at the fire, appraising the situation with a practiced glance.

"I believe the mortal is comfortable where she is," Coal tells Tye. "Would you like me to sit on your lap instead as a consolation prize?"

I'm about to push myself up and sit in my own bloody space when the air a few paces away ripples in a familiar motion. Like watching steam billow from a pot. My hand tightens against Shade's arm, digging into his flesh with what has to be painful force—though he gives no sign of being bothered.

"Last supper?" Klarissa says, stepping gingerly over loose stones. Despite the late hour, the female looks as spectacular as when I last saw her. Her dress, a formfitting silk the color of bitter chocolate, shimmers like liquid gold in the firelight. The flames likewise catch on Klarissa's topaz brooch and earrings, the latter swaying rhythmically under their great weight. She sniffs the air, her nostrils flaring delicately. "There is no reason to be afraid anymore, Leralynn. You will be safe now that you've found the presence of mind to call me."

I glance at River, my mouth suddenly dry.

River stays just as he was, ignoring my gaze. Right. This part is on me.

Pushing myself away from Shade, I stride up to the female and bow deeply. "I cannot thank you enough for coming, Elder," I say, holding the bow piously. "The males are doing their best, but they can't keep me safe the way you could."

Klarissa's face dissolves into a benevolent smile and she

holds a slender hand out to me. "Tell me what you want, child."

I straighten, taking the offered hand. "Please take Pyker away."

Klarissa's face freezes. "Pyker?"

River gets to his feet, his hands clasped behind his back as he shakes his head and comes to stand beside me. "That male attempted to murder Leralynn. We caught the rogue, of course, but Pyker's very presence frightens her still. We explained ten times over that the bastard can't hurt her anymore, but Leralynn insisted we call you. Said there is no one she trusts more to deal with the traitor."

Icy silence settles over the clearing, the crackling fire trying and failing to dispel the chill. I release Klarissa's hand and feel Coal step up behind me, stopping opposite River on my other side. Then Tye. A light flashes in the corner of my vision and Shade's wolf trots up as well, yawning lazily as he stretches out before my feet, blocking the path between Klarissa and me. Even without us all touching, the power of five pulses through my veins, waking the strength inside me.

Klarissa clears her throat, her hands smoothing her wrinkle-free dress. "The males can take care of Pyker, Leralynn. Let me take you home first, and then I promise you that the traitor will be dealt with severely."

I raise my chin. "Home?" My voice is clear and loud as it pierces the night, my heart punctuating each syllable. "I am already home, Elder. Home is wherever my quint is."

"Oh, blessed stars," Klarissa throws up her hands and wheels on River, her eyes dismissing me like a newly noticed piece of rubbish. "Enough of this, River. We are not in Slait Court any longer, and there is no more jurisdictional conflict.

Explain to the mortal what must be done and let us spare everyone the trip to the Citadel."

"I already explained, Elder. Leralynn and the others all understand the requirement that we renew our oath before the full council." There is nothing kind in River's smile. "Unless the rest of the council has vested you with the power to accept our oath yourself?"

"The oath?" Klarissa's hand tightens into a fist. "You will take the oath with this . . . creature?"

"Yes," says River, adding after a heartbeat, "You've always had astute observational skills, Klarissa. It appears this evening is no exception."

Klarissa's eyes flash and she takes a step forward.

Shade's wolf growls.

Klarissa stops, her eyes alight with murder. "Present your quint to the Citadel, River. We shall talk again then," she says, biting off each word before turning her back to us and stalking toward the camp's edge, her hips swaying. "Fetch me Pyker, one of you," she calls over her shoulder, snapping her fingers in emphasis. "I've no more time to waste here."

33

LERALYNN

*W*ith our future settled, at least as far as the coming week is concerned, I discover a new question now looming over the quint. One that is taking an absurd amount of time to debate, especially considering the late hour.

"I've slept with her every night," Shade says, raising his chin. "There is no reason to change what works."

"That is utterly unjust," says Tye.

"How about I just sleep by myself, like I've done every night for twenty years?" I say, finally injecting myself into the conversation.

"No," the four say together.

"At least you agree on something," I mutter.

"We would all feel safer if one of us sleeps by your side, Leralynn," River says in too-patient tones for the tenth time in as many minutes. If I thought the males protective before, my official agreement to join the quint has deteriorated their behavior to new levels.

"And I would feel safer if you didn't kill each other." I throw up my hands. "Can we pull straws? Take turns? Do anything but a combat to the death?"

"Straws," Shade agrees.

"Turns," says Tye.

"I'm fine with combat," says Coal.

I grab a cloak off the ground, not caring whose it was originally. "I am going to sleep," I declare, stalking around to the other side of the partition. I build myself a thick nest of pine branches, then lay the cloak on top of it to lie on while the others continue arguing. The pallet made, I lower my body into its sweet, sappy arms, letting the day's memories sing their strange lullaby to my thoughts.

The voices on the other side of the rock become distant, my body so deeply surrendering to fatigue that I don't know which of them finally lies down beside me, or how long I was asleep before it happened. I just know that the warm, muscular body at my back is one of my males, and that alone sends a wave of heat through me. Intensely enough to have me clenching my thighs despite the all-consuming slumber.

I wake some hours later to a star-filled sky and a feeling of being watched. The feeling, I quickly discover upon turning around to find a pair of amused green eyes, is all too justified.

"What are you doing, Tye?" I mutter.

"Listening to those little delicious sounds you make when you sleep."

My face heats as my vivid dreams return to me. "I don't make sounds," I say, sitting up to survey the rest of the campsite. The fire has burned its course, leaving several handfuls of embers still glowing red in the dark. The remains of dinner seem to have been cleared away, and the place seems empty. I tilt my head, listening for the telltale breathing of other beings, but hear only the quiet rush of the miniature waterfall.

"If you are wondering whether anyone else heard the sounds you weren't making, the answer is no," says Tye, stretching his arms. He's wearing breeches and a thin shirt, the long muscles along his ribs shifting slightly beneath the cloth. "River wanted to sweep the forest and Gloom, make sure that Klarissa didn't leave any surprises for us. He took Coal and the fur ball with him."

"Do you think she did leave any surprises?"

"Unlikely. We'll be at the Citadel soon enough, and she'll take us by the bollocks then." Tye moves closer and nudges me to lie back down. When I shake my head, he drapes an arm around me and lowers us to the pallet together, his hand stroking my hair. "Go back to sleep, Lilac Girl," Tye whispers. "You are safe."

I curl up on my side, my forehead pressed against Tye's chest, and close my eyes. Open them a minute later. Close them again. "I don't want to sleep," I say finally, rolling onto my back to look at the stars.

Tye rises onto his elbow. "And what do you want?" he asks, his green eyes sparkling as he blows a slow, cool breath over the top of my hair, sending a soft shiver down my skin and very unsavory answers to his question through my mind.

I touch my scalp first, then extend a finger to trace across Tye's lips. "Was that . . ."

"Magic?" Tye grins. "Yes. Fire magic can take heat away as well. I'm not very strong on that part, but it's enough." He blows softly into my ear, this one hot and cold by turn.

My toes curl. The fact that I know the bastard is teasing me is of no help in calming my quickening pulse. "Enough to trick the air?"

"Enough to get me into trouble," says Tye. He groans, turning onto his back and intently tucking his arms behind his head. Despite the appearance of a relaxed posture, Tye's lithe body sings with a tension that my own treacherous flesh answers in kind.

I squirm to relieve the ache growing ever more insistent between my legs.

"You really should sleep." Tye winces, his voice tight. "Quietly, if you can."

Right. Of course. I cross my thighs, which helps a bit with the insistently pulsing need, and turn away from the warrior. The pine branches poke my side and I shimmy in the makeshift pallet to find a comfortable spot.

"Lilac Girl," Tye says through gritted teeth, his body vibrating slightly. "Don't do that."

"Do what?" I flip over, rising on one elbow. My better sense has plainly gone to sleep without the rest of me, because instead of doing as Tye asks, I walk my finger over his chest, smiling as his muscles shudder beneath my touch. Playing with fire. Because while my body is quite explicit in what it would like, it doesn't actually know how to get there. It's never gone . . . *there* before. And I'm not sure how to tell someone like Tye *that* little problem, but maybe we could skip the talking. I run a nail across his nipple.

Tye growls, pouncing like a cat from the pallet beneath us. My breath catches as he flattens me onto my back and braces his body over mine, his powerful arms extended, his palms anchored on either side of my head. Tye's flop of red hair falls from his face, tickling my cheeks. He grinds his pelvis into mine lightly. "What do you want?" Tye asks softly, his mouth and chest hovering above me, close but not touching. "Tell me, Lilac Girl."

"You." The truth spills out, sending my heart into a gallop. I've not had a man before, and this male above me . . . If the sheer size of his chest and shoulders is any indication of what I'll find between his powerful thighs, I should be frightened right now. Except I'm not. I feel like I can't be frightened of Tye, or any of the quint. Not because they are not dangerous —they are predators through their blood and soul—but because when I'm with them, I'm a predator too. "You," I say again, this time certain of my words as my body shudders in confirmation.

Tye grins, the tip of his tongue flickering over his elongated canines. "And what shall I do with you?" he muses, that gleam in his eyes taking in my body, lingering appreciatively on my chest and hips before returning to my eyes. Tye bends his elbows, bringing his body flush with mine, though his weight remains on his hands. His head lowers until the tips of those canines nip my earlobe.

I squirm and Tye chuckles into my ear. "Never mind, Lilac Girl. I'll decide."

He flexes, straightening his arms and rolling off me, his right leg resting possessively between my thighs while his free hand pulls at the laces of my shirt, which obediently falls open to expose my stomach. "You really should marvel at my restraint," he says, running his fingers along my collarbone. "These clothes are in the way of my plans for your body, and I've yet to destroy them."

He brushes his hand lightly along my side, curving around the bend of my hip before returning to my skin. Tye's strong, dexterous fingers trace a circle around my bellybutton and then, just when I'm about to giggle, slip under the waistband of my pants.

My breath catches, my thighs longing to press together to

control a different type of tingling, but Tye's deftly positioned leg allows no such escape. His fingers graze lower, then lower still. A little more and there will be no hiding the wetness building between my legs. He's trapped me. Expertly. Exquisitely. Excruciatingly. "Tye—"

"So much talking," he chides, bringing his painfully handsome face close enough to mine to nip my lip gently. My mouth opens to emit a gasp, which is all the male needs to press his velvet lips against mine. The kiss starts quick and teasing, but then I press back into him and a tremor runs through Tye's body. He deepens the kiss, claiming my mouth as his hand under my waistband discovers my secret.

Tye pulls away, grinning as he licks his fingers one at a time, each flick of his tongue making the heat inside me flare.

"What . . . about your clothes?" My voice is raspy, too much of my attention drawn low on my body. "I little like them either."

Tye chuckles once, reaching around back and pulling his shirt obediently over his head. Muscles honed through years of battle shift beneath smooth skin. I place both my palms on his sculpted chest, which expands with starved breaths above me. When my finger touches Tye's nipple again, he uncoils suddenly, lifting my shoulders with one hand and deftly liberating me of my chest band.

Clearly, the male has done this before. I, on the other hand . . .

"You are perfect," Tye whispers as if reading the worry in my eyes. "You are more than perfect, Lilac Girl. You are an exquisite being, and I will savor exploring every secret of this wicked body of yours. And then, when I'm done with that . . ." He gives me a feline grin.

"And then?" I breathe.

Tye brings his lips close to my ear, nipping the earlobe as his hand slides right back under my waistband, this time finding its target without delay. "And then," Tye whispers, his mouth still at my ear while his fingers slide leisurely along my sex, forward and back, forward and back, forward and—

I buck as Tye's touch stops just outside my opening, teasing it gleefully while I writhe, not knowing whether I want to kiss him or kill him. "And then you'll decide just how deep the exploration should go. But we'll save that little tidbit for next time."

"What?" I whimper. "Why?"

Tye's fingers trail away, flicking over my apex instead. For an instant, I want to scream at the inadequate consolation prize, but with the next heartbeat my eyes widen, my hips undulating at the sudden deluge of heat his tiny touches bring, and I want to scream for a different reason entirely. My sex pulses, Tye's finger moving faster and faster. His *finger.* Just the thought of what would happen if he entered . . . if his cock entered . . . The phantom fullness makes me shudder even as the very real rhythm of Tye's touch pushes me over the edge I've been skimming. My body arches up to the sky, surrendering to an explosion of pleasure.

I pant, staring at Tye as he withdraws his hand from my sex and brushes it along my neck, my collarbone, the swell of my breast. "There are five of us, Lilac Girl. And the lesser three would never forgive us if we left them out of our first joining."

The End

Continue the adventure in *Mistake of Magic, Power of Five Book 2*.

Reviews are a book's lifeblood. Please support Lera's story by reviewing this book on Amazon. Just one sentence helps a lot.

ALSO BY ALEX LIDELL

SIGN UP FOR NEW RELEASE NOTIFICATIONS at
www.subscribepage.com/TIDES

ABOUT THE AUTHOR

Alex Lidell is the Amazon Breakout Novel Awards finalist author of THE CADET OF TILDOR (Penguin, 2013). She is an avid horseback rider, a (bad) hockey player, and an ice-cream addict. Born in Russia, Alex learned English in elementary school, where a thoughtful librarian placed a copy of Tamora Pierce's ALANNA in Alex's hands. In addition to becoming the first English book Alex read for fun, ALANNA started Alex's life long love for fantasy books. Alex lives in Washington, DC. Join Alex's newsletter for news, bonus content and sneak peeks: www.subscribepage.com/TIDES Find out more on Alex's website: www.alexlidell.com

SIGN UP FOR NEWS AND RELEASE NOTIFICATIONS

Connect with Alex!
www.alexlidell.com
alex@alexlidell.com

Made in the USA
Las Vegas, NV
21 June 2024

91318538R00132